Mama's House

Book 2 of Mama Series

By Patricia Strefling

Mama's House
Book 2 of Mama Series
Written by Patricia Strefling
Copyright © 2015 by Patricia Strefling
Graphics, book cover and formatting by Leah Banicki

http://www.patriciastrefling.com/

On Facebook:
https://www.facebook.com/patricia.strefling.author

Patricia Strefling's blog: http://patriciastrefling.blogspot.com/

Note from the Author

Hush Mama and *Mama's House* are works of fiction. However, for ˙ my historical readers I want to mention that I have taken the liberty of using an actual event in Charleston's history twenty-one years before it happened. Charleston experienced the worst earthquake in its history in 1886 at 9:50 p.m. August 31st. All the facts are true about the earthquake, except the placement in my fictional story in 1865.

Acknowledgements

Every writer needs the work of several sets of eyes to make a story better. I would like to thank C.J. Batterson and Leslie Risner for their time reading and contributing their ideas and to Karalee Johnson for the wonderful final edit. Without each of your unique gifts I would be lost.

Prologue

Thankfully, with the end of the Civil War, 1865 is drawing to a close.

The New Year brings with it new hopes and dreams. The south is beginning to rebuild. Karalee knows, come Spring, Mother will be returning to her ancestral home, Charleston. She hopes to get Mother settled and return to Michigan. Gazing out at the snow-covered scene, Karalee's thoughts turn to leaving her childhood home and all the memories here.

Thus far it seemed her lot in life was to lose the people she loved most. First John, her elder brother, then Father and now Jackson? The day Father left to bring her wounded brother home from the war, Karalee had promised him she'd be strong, no matter what happened. She had never imagined that would involve both of them dying. How could she let Father and John down and now perhaps lose Jackson, the only man who had made a declaration of love to her?

The snow, its silent, brilliant presence, sent shivers down her arms. Brooding, she pulled her knitted shawl around her more tightly. Karalee knew it wasn't just the snow, but fear of losing the man who had saved her from the evil intentions of Mr. Jasper Rutledge. The fragile connection she and Jackson Woodridge had, seemed to be falling apart. His sweet sister Lily, had encouraged her. But if she left now, she might never know if he truly meant what he said.

She would miss her neighbor Laura who had become Mother's caretaker. Her friend Julianne had foolishly attached herself to that ruthless and manipulative Mr. Rutledge. Who would be here to look after her?

Baffled by the turn of events in her life, Karalee pulled the heavy curtains closed and turned. Mother was calling.

One

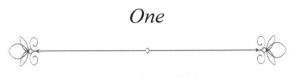

December 1865

"Karalee, come quickly, there is word from Mother and Father."

Karalee pulled off her apron and rushed to her mother's side. She had not heard the post arrive.

"Your hair is mussed," Mother complained and slit open the envelope with a quickness Karalee hadn't seen in weeks. Laura was adjusting the drapes over Mother's bed to let in more light.

The fragrance of lavender hung in the air after Mother's bath. The scent conjured up old memories of Saturday nights when she and her elder brother John took turns bathing in the old tin tub. Tiredness crept over Karalee as she smoothed her hair and sat down in the chair at Mother's bedside.

"Laura, please leave us," Mother ordered, to which the kind young woman smiled and said, "Yes, Mrs. Williams."

"Mother, why must you be so unkind?" Karalee whispered when Laura had slipped out of the room. "She is doing her best to take care of you."

"Laura knows her place." Mother shushed her with a wave of her hand.

Karalee was glad to rest for a few minutes. Once Mother had made a decision, there was only the goal ahead to be spoken of until it came to pass. Then she admonished herself. There was news from her beloved grandparents. At least they had survived this horrendous war.

Mother unfolded the letter, pressed the creases with firm resolve and held it up to the light from the window. The December snowfall was especially dreadful this year in Michigan, but Karalee reminded herself they were headed to Charleston and to warmer weather. Her mind wandered and then was brought back with a firm tap to her forearm.

Mother must have full attention. She began to read and Karalee closed her eyes and listened. Mother read on about the devastation the South had suffered at the hands of the Union. Bitterness welled up in her eyes as she stopped and gave Karalee a look.

Life had been hard, but not as hard as staying away from their beloved home, Granmama Drayton wrote. Mother huffed and said, "Well, those Yankees best get back on their own side, all the damage they've done to our landholdings we worked to build." She clicked her tongue.

"Mother, we are a united nation now," Karalee stated, yet felt torn. Everywhere, people were hurting. The Southerners, Northerners, and Slaves recently declared free by President Lincoln's Proclamation. So many fathers and sons, husbands and brothers lost. Had all their deaths made a difference?

Too tired to think of it, she waited as Mother paused and read silently. Karalee watched her face, hoping there was no more bad news. She waited, squeezing her hands tighter in her lap.

"Father is ill," Mother said and let her hands, the letter crushed in them, fall into her lap.

Karalee looked up and saw two tears drop from her mother's eyes. "It's not good, Lee-Lee."

Karalee held her gaze. "You have not called me that...in forever." Karalee's heart softened at the endearment and knew how much Mother loved Grandaddy. Mother, his first-born, strong-willed, and only daughter was his favorite. Samuel who came along four years after Mama, had been a sickly child, and had never walked the way Grandaddy expected. He married and moved away. Mother said Samuel was weak as a kitten and never could stand up to his own wife.

And then there was Henderson, born six years after Samuel. Mother was ten by then. Karalee remembered him as a rugged, handsome, fearless young man. He had Mama's black hair and blue eyes. Karalee last saw him when he was seventeen and even as a young girl, knew he was wildly independent. As the youngest, he had the most impulsive drive. He left in 1849 to chase after gold in California and had not been heard from since.

"There is no word from Samuel or Henderson," Mother collected herself and was reading again. "Pray to God they come home if they

6

have any sense," she said firmly, "for I am in no condition to run the plantation alone."

Karalee agreed. "Would it be better to wait and see if they are home before we go down?" She reminded her that the Drayton house may not have survived the war. So many plantations and mansions had been burned or destroyed in battle.

One look from Mother's hard blue eyes gave her the answer. She stood when Mother said that was the end of the letter. Karalee took the envelope and looked it over. Granmama's shaky handwriting made her smile. That alone brought back memories of days past. Surely Grandaddy and Granmama were, in their old age, worn thin with having to leave their beloved home to live on the edge of the Mason-Dixon line—on the *wrong* side as Mother put it—and wonder if their stately Charleston home on the one-hundred-four acre rice plantation, *Magnolia Breeze*, was intact.

"Mother, at least you are safe," she reminded her.

"Safe? I have never felt safe up here in the North," she spit out.

"You are alive."

"Oh Karalee, you are so dreary. You always were. I declare, you need to gather up some backbone."

Karalee had heard *that* before and chose to ignore it. The thing was she *did* have backbone. Enough to help Jackson with his abolitionist work, all without her Mother's knowledge.

No matter what, she and Mother would never agree when it came to how they lived their lives. Sadly, Karalee had decided long ago she did not wish to be like Mother. Father was the only one who understood her and he was gone. John, her beloved older brother, had loved her best. He used to tease her, repeating Mother's negative words, until one day he heard Mother speaking of him in the same manner. After that John never teased her again.

Suddenly, she could not stay in the room. "I'm going back to work."

Mother waved her off and then called out, "Send Laura back."

Karalee pulled on her coat, walked next door and asked if Laura might return after she had finished her lunch and any duties she may have to her own family. Mother would be furious Laura had not rushed right to her, but so be it.

7

Just back from a short walk, Karalee heard the rattle of Jackson's wagon coming down the road. She hadn't seen him in days. He drove slowly, the snow high around the spoked wheels.

She waited on the front veranda, her wool coat wrapped tightly around her. She hadn't thought to grab a shawl for her head. Her mind had been elsewhere.

When he stopped at the front walk, she made her way to the black wrought iron gate surrounding the house and opened it.

He greeted her with warm brown eyes, his face reddened by the cold. Town was just a few blocks down the way. "Supplies?"

"Yep." He pulled off his hat and snapped it against his leg, scattering snow in the wind before he put it back on.

"Are you all right?" She gazed at him, feeling her heart flutter at his presence.

He nodded.

She had learned long ago Jackson Clay Woodridge was a man of few words. "Is Lily well?"

"Yes," he said rather gruffly and handed her a note. "From Lily." The soft gazes they had shared just weeks ago were different now. He didn't look deep into her eyes the way he had before. And for the life of her, Karalee didn't know why. She looked down at her snow-covered shoes. She hadn't thought to put on her boots.

Perhaps he had changed his mind about her. Heaven knows, she wouldn't blame him. She had messed up everything she had touched when they worked together. First, she had discovered hidden slaves at his place, then almost got them caught once. And now that she and Mother were going to Charleston, maybe he regretted having said once that he loved her.

Thoughts flew through her mind. She looked away for a moment and felt the heavy snow gathering up in her hair. "I must get inside," she said, giving him his freedom. He had come on the wishes of his sister.

"Right." He pricked his hat with his thumb and forefinger and nodded, walked back out in the snow, climbed on the wagon and drove away slowly.

Karalee wanted to cry. Had she been wrong in seeing love in those same dark eyes once, not too many weeks ago?

Two

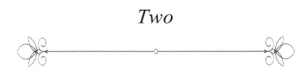

Unwelcome tears ran down Karalee's cold face—partly because Granddaddy Drayton was ill, partly because she didn't know what to think about Jackson, and partly because she was just plain weary. The people she loved most no longer existed, at least in *this* world. She was tired of losing. Stomping her feet off on the veranda, she slipped inside and heard Mother's frustrated call.

"Yes, Mother," she said walking to her door, forcing herself to hold her tongue.

"Go hang up your coat. You are dripping snow on my good floor," she admonished and waved her away, then called out, "Is Laura on her way?"

Karalee ignored her for the moment as she hung her coat. She needed one bit of peace before she walked back into her room. Mama's house was a solemn one. Once all was in order to her satisfaction, Karalee marched to the kitchen and brought wood in to warm up the two fireplaces on the main floor. All the doors had been shut to the unused rooms, to keep the heat centralized.

Just as she added the last log to Mother's fireplace, already having done so in the parlor, she heard Laura tap, come through the door, hang up her coat and go straight to Mother's room.

"Laura is going to read, Karalee. If you wish, you may take a nap. You seem a bit under the weather...and for sure *you* must not get sick else I shall suffer."

Gone was the "Lee-Lee" Mother had called her just a few minutes ago. A nap was exactly what she needed. She felt like a spoiled child. The world was not going right for her and she was pouting. Up the stairs she went, the sound of fresh wood popping as the fire ate it up. The loft space was perfect. Father built two rooms up there, one for her, one for John. And now Julianne had moved into town, which reminded Karalee: she needed to stop by and see how her

9

friend was faring in the presence of one Mr. Jasper Adolphus Rutledge.

Karalee sighed, thankful she had been saved from the grips of *that* man, then instantly recalled that he had more than paid for his follies. Feeling torn between her unkind thoughts and gratefulness that Jackson had saved her from Rutledge, she lay down and without another thought, slept.

The next thing she remembered was waking to a wonderful aroma. Chicken soup? Laura must have brought a chicken. After a quick trip to the downstairs lavatory, she made her way to the kitchen. There sat Laura at the old wooden table, studying a book.

"Oh, you're up," Laura said kindly. "Did you rest well?"

"Yes. Thank you for allowing me to nap."

"You've been quite busy." She smiled knowingly.

"Indeed, I have. Is it ready?" Karalee stirred the pot of broth. "Oh, dumplings, too? How do you manage, Laura?"

She shrugged and placed a small piece of brown paper in the book and shut it.

"You love learning, do you not?"

"I do. Doc gave me one of his old medical books. You know how many parts of the brain it takes just to move your finger, let alone walk?" Laura's blue eyes were large.

Karalee pulled down one of Mother's bowls and served Laura then herself. "Let's enjoy this blustery winter day," Karalee said, grateful they had food, a good neighbor, and were still alive, even if there were struggles. Laura put her spoon down and prayed a short prayer as they always did, then told Karalee all about the miracle of the human brain in relation to one's body.

Later, after dishes were washed and set aside to dry, Laura went in to read to Mother while Karalee packed more boxes. Most of Father's belongings were to be stored in whatever trunks they could find and put into the barn. Father's things would not be going to Charleston. Mother had no idea, but Karalee fully intended to return in a few months, once Mother was settled. Someone had to care for the house that Father built. Mother would be furious. She expected Karalee to stay and help run the plantation. But she was no longer a child. Besides, if, and this was a big if...Karalee had to know if Jackson still cared for her.

* * *

Several days later the clock gong struck noon and Karalee had just finished packing the last of Father's things, including all his books, except a few she kept aside to read. Those were mostly fiction stories…something that would take away the feeling of hopelessness. Sorting through Father's papers had ripped every memory from the past and replanted them fresh in her head, until she was nothing but a mess. Mother was sing-song happy these days and Karalee, even after hearing Pastor's Sunday sermons on love and forgiveness, was still prickly-tempered.

She and Jackson were no longer working together, Julianne was not available, Mother was her usual self, and Karalee was taking orders left and right to get the house closed up. She had thanked God numerous times for Laura. That was her only prayer these days it seemed.

She had tried several times to let Mother know she would be coming back, but somehow had never quite found the strength to say it firmly. Every time she did mention anything near to it, Mother resounded with, "You will stay with me, Karalee. And that is the end of it."

Karalee knew she would not.

But if Jackson felt differently than before, Karalee knew she could *not* possibly stay in Cassopolis.

Three

Christmas was days away. The snow had stopped and the ground was covered in perfectly white low-rolling hills, untouched by man or beast. Stores stayed open late for shoppers, the newly installed gaslights brightening up the town considerably. The small city was awhirl with school plays, dinners, and church services.

Mother had announced she was not going to accept a single invitation. She had too much to think about. Karalee knew it was because of the shooting incident. Most of Mother's friends had "deserted" her. The ones who did drop by for visits were turned away. There were no more card games or delightful afternoon teas. Mother had burned her bridges.

Karalee found visits to the quiet barn to see Rosebud in the evenings a solace, even in the colder weather. While she was brushing her horse, something suddenly dashed through her spirit. Memories began to surface.

Lily and Jackson had stayed for supper... sad thing was Jackson said he needed to leave early because of an obligation. Foolishly, Karalee had wondered if he had found another woman he wished to pursue: one much more worthy and with more to offer than she could ever give.

Then another thought flashed through her mind making her angry. *She had been fixing a plate for Jackson to take home, via Mother's duty to her guests, and found he was standing in the kitchen with her, alone.*

Karalee had felt her face burn when she turned and saw him quickly drop his gaze...her heart beating a bit faster. "Chicken, ham or both?" *She had filled the air with a sensible question.*

"*Both.*"

She had layered the food in a linen-lined cigar box from her father's desk, wrapped the box in dark paper, tied it with a string and handed it to him, purposely not looking him in the eye. She had not wanted to see disappointment...again.

"Thanks."

"You're welcome," she had answered the same way he spoke, curt, to the point.

He had hesitated...Karalee could see he wanted to say something. "What is it Jackson?" She had turned to him and said, "We're alone, we can talk."

He had nodded, gazed into her eyes with that dark look of his...she could see his mind working.

"Never mind," he had said abruptly, slowly backed up, and then turned, putting his hat on as he walked away. Karalee had had a sick feeling—this would be the last she would see of Jackson Woodridge.

* * *

Karalee continued brushing Rosebud's coat, glad to keep her hands busy while memories rolled in like storm clouds.

Jackson had had the chance to speak and didn't. Karalee had realized he didn't trust her...why would he? She had proven to be just as her mother said: foolish and unwise in not choosing a man to take care of her, and...when Mother passed, what then?

Guilt, regret and fear had bundled up and stuffed itself down her throat. She had hated it, but there it was; she was a woman who could have presented herself to one of the local men at a decent age, dressed like a man wanted a woman to look, and showed she was clever enough to run a household. Now without father, brother, and one day mother, she wondered if, when she thought herself free and wise, she may have played the fool.

That evening she had cleared her head with a shake and heard Lily saying her goodbyes. She needed to see them out, had pinched her cheeks and lifted her head...she did have some of Mother's determination. With a genuine look of gratefulness to Lily and to Jackson, she'd wished them Happy Christmas.

Karalee had pushed the door shut and with it, a new resolve formed in her mind. She'd put Mother to bed, turned out her lights, and started to add logs to the fire for overnight. Then she saw

Jackson had already done it... and left a log near all the chimneys in case it became cold through the night.

Her heart had softened a bit; Jackson was a good man...if he didn't have feelings for her like he thought, well, so be it. For the first time in several days, she had prayed on her knees at her bedside, "God if you want me with Jackson, show me the way. If not, show me what you want of me. I must have a purpose or I shall perish."

Karalee forced the memories away, fed Rosebud and went inside. She would have to trust that God had heard her prayer.

* * *

Morning came with a crash. Someone was in the kitchen. Karalee grabbed her wrapper and slipped down the stairs.

"Mother what are you doing up?"

"Making my plum pudding. Christmas is three days away."

"But there will be just the two of us," Karalee said firmly. "Besides, you have not been in the kitchen in weeks. What do you mean getting out of bed and taking the chance you will fall again?"

"I know what I can do," Mother said crossly. "Now move out of my way. I am weak from lying about, but I am not helpless."

Karalee stepped aside with a slight smile and wondered at her change of attitude. Mother would always be Mother. At least she was on her feet, limping about, but up. Leaving Mother to her duties, she went upstairs, wrote in her journal and slipped it back into its hiding place. Sun shone through her window. Finally the darkness of the past few days' snowstorm had gone away.

She chose a simple housedress and thought perhaps she and Mother might have English tea, a gift from Julianne. The minute she was dressed, had adjusted her stockings and put on soft slippers, she heard the door knocker and Mother's strong voice to "Come at once!"

Karalee made a quick descent and, heart beating, wondered if perhaps Jackson had stopped by again. She opened the door with a smile and caught her breath: Timothy and Ruth Thompson.

"Please come in." She hoped they did not detect her disappointment.

Karalee stepped aside, shut the door against the cold and welcomed them into the parlor, then added another log to the fire.

"It is a beautiful day," she remarked as she worked.

"It is indeed," Mrs. Thompson agreed.

"I will get Mother," she said and hurried to the kitchen.

"Who was at the door, Karalee?"

"Mr. and Mrs. Thompson. I'll get tea. Have we any pastries left?"

"Just enough. Here put them on this plate. It looks nicer." Mother handed her a large plate with a Christmas theme. I'll bring tea in a minute or two. I must finish this and put it in the oven."

"Don't be long, Mother." Karalee said and made her way to the parlor.

"Oh my goodness. We must not stay," Mrs. Thompson said quickly, "Nor bother your Mother. She is not yet well?"

"She is much better," Karalee assured her and hoped they might stay for a few more minutes. Mr. Thompson looked very uncomfortable. Mother would approve of his beard. Grandaddy always had a beard. This house needed a bit of a lift. Mother came, limping slowly yet elegantly around the corner, her best shawl wrapped around her shoulders, looking every bit the part of a Southern woman, oozing with genuine hospitality.

"Why, I have seen you pass in the wagon all fall and winter." Mother greeted them. "How is your farm?"

"It is well. It is good to see you, Mrs. Williams," Ruth said quietly. "We have been praying for you," she added as she accepted her hostess' cup of tea.

Mother didn't exactly believe that prayer worked. Karalee's quick glance and a slight dip of her chin warned Mother not to say a word.

A few minutes later, Mr. Thompson stood and said he had work to do outside and would leave the women to talk while he went on an errand. Karalee saw him to the door and heard his wagon pull away. Quakers never sat still for long, she remembered.

After some time in conversation followed by a few quiet moments, Mother's southern hospitality surfaced again and she brought out some bread slathered with butter and apricot jam. Karalee's eyes opened wider as she smiled. Mother was serving her best jam.

A good hour passed and soon Mr. Thompson was stomping his feet on the veranda and calling for his wife. They left with a tip of his

15

hat and a twinkle in Mrs. Thompson's eye. Somehow, it felt a little more like Christmas.

Four

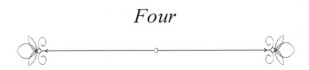

That same afternoon after the Thompson visit, Mother asked for lard from the smokehouse. She had a need to "work up an apricot cake." Karalee, happy to oblige Mother's desire to cook, did her bidding and headed for the smokehouse, reached for the wooden spoon, pulled down the cloth-covered wood bucket and gasped. The entire space was filled with meat hanging from hooks. Ham, deer, turkey and marked packages wrapped in dark butcher paper were stacked on the shelves.

She stared and knew instantly: The Thompsons. They barely knew them. It must have been Jackson or Lily who mentioned they were low on food.

Karalee felt her heart swing from despair to joy. They would have enough for months. Their food supply had been low because Karalee was helping Jackson feed the slaves. There had been so many, but how could they let them starve?

She knew just enough about the Thompsons to know they had been helping Jackson for years, and finally retired, having plenty to do at their farm. They came out of retirement only when emergencies arose.

Now this. Should she tell Mother about the food? How could she not? Perhaps Mother would see God not only hears prayers, but *answers* them as well. She spooned the lard, took down a small package of deer sausage and carried it inside.

"Mother, are you up to stepping outside to the smokehouse?"

"Whatever for, child?" she asked.

"I want to show you something."

"What is it?" she grumped.

Karalee put the package on the table. "Where did that come from?" Mother's blue eyes looked bluer in the sun-filled kitchen.

"Come see for yourself."

Not one to miss something unusual, Mother took her shawl off the hook, wrapped it around herself tightly and slipped on an old pair of shoes by the back door, then winced as she walked slowly on her bad leg.

"Well, I'll be. Where did all this come from?" She looked at her daughter with a slight lift of her chin. You know we don't accept charity. I won't have anyone thinking..."

"Mother," Karalee interrupted her, "who would know? No one comes here. There's no one to impress anymore."

Mother gave her a stern look and shrugged. "Well, see to it this does not oblige us to be indebted to anyone," she admonished.

"It's a gift, Mother. No one is going to come and take it back or make us pay for it."

"Do you suppose it was that Quaker couple?"

"Of course it was. Mr. Thompson went out and unloaded his wagon. And he did it without us knowing. They have pigs, you know, and he makes the best deer sausage this side of the Mississippi."

"I wouldn't agree with that...why, we have the best venison on *that* side of the Mississippi." She pointed south.

"No matter," Karalee said quietly. "We have been given a gift. Let us invite someone for Christmas, Mother. Someone who doesn't have much. Let's share with others."

"There you go again, resting on your feelings. It would be better..."

Her Mother stopped short and Karalee knew she was thinking of something that would suit her own interests. It took only a moment.

"Mother, do not plan to invite some available gentleman to sit next to me at the table."

"Karalee, that Jackson boy doesn't come around much. He may be well off, but a suitable marriage with a gentleman would do nicely, especially if you are foolishly thinking of staying here," she declared.

"Mother, I will choose whom I marry. We are not going through this again. You see what happened with Mr. Rutledge. That's the end of it!" Now she sounded just like Mother. "Come let's go in and talk about who we might invite. I'm thinking we can give Laura's large family first chance. They have done so much for us."

18

"There is a man at the head of that family. They are fine, Karalee. Think of someone else. I will not feed seven mouths when the man can do it himself."

It was impossible to fall in with Mama, so Karalee decided to keep her thoughts to herself for the moment and waited for what she knew would be Mother's reply.

"I am tired. Overworked, what with unannounced company, cooking and walking. Doc said not to work my leg too hard. Might get a blood clot."

"You're right. Go back inside and take a nap. I'll make some sausage and potato soup."

"Good idea." Mother handed her the package of meat she was holding and went inside, the apricot cake forgotten.

Karalee stood in the smokehouse for a few minutes looking at the gifts the Thompsons had left, then headed toward the house, and noticed that the woodpile had increased by half. Timothy Thompson, an older man, had delivered that wood. Karalee couldn't help the tears that flooded her eyes and prayed for Timothy and Ruth. She remembered they were deep-down good folks that had risked their lives and livelihood helping the slaves escape. Jackson had mentioned that once in passing. She had not forgotten.

A sudden sense of purpose was growing up inside of her again. Time to make someone else's Christmas as blessed as theirs had already been. She prayed a prayer, "Lord, show me the way."

Immediately she thought of Julianne. They could invite her away from what must be a very dull household, since Mr. Rutledge was probably even more difficult, now that he was unable to walk. And she *would* invite Laura's family. Mother would have to put up with it.

Would Lily and Jackson come if she asked?

No, that would be like pressing Jackson for his attention. She decided against that at once. If Jackson wanted her, he would have to come for her. She had not moved, he had.

They only had two days to prepare. Karalee made a mental list of a possible meal plan. As she stepped inside the door, she saw Mother had left her cookbook on the table with a note: *I will make biscuits in the morning.*

Karalee pulled in a deep breath and let it out. It was amazing how a single act of kindness could renew one's spirit. Mother had been

19

touched too, even if she didn't realize it. Hope crept in and pushed out the dark thoughts she had been entertaining these past weeks.

Life was how one saw it could be rather than how it was at present. She wrote that in her journal and didn't go check on Mother, but went straight up to bed with a pencil and paper to write down a dinner plan. First thing on the list was turkey and Mother's special Southern recipe for dressing.

Five

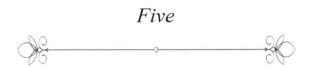

The next two days were spent preparing. Karalee asked Laura's eldest brother, Jonas, to act as currier to deliver her hastily made invitations and gave him a silver dollar for his efforts. The snow had stopped at least and folks would be able to make it down the hard frozen dirt road into town. Everyone had accepted. Jonas had chanced to meet Lily on the way and excitedly told her of the plans the Misses Williams had. Jonas had returned with a private note from Lily asking for Karalee to please invite them, hinting Jackson had been struggling lately and not to think too harshly of him at this time. Karalee considered her words and wrote a note back, then apologized to Jonas for his having to make a second trip. She slipped several coins into his hand and knew immediately, Jonas did not mind at all.

A woman knows when a man is stepping away, Karalee thought with a knot in her stomach. If Jackson Clay Woodridge did not wish to be with her, she would not ensnare him. She knew the feeling of being the rabbit in a trap. No, God would have to be in charge of this. She had work to do and set to getting plans underway.

She and Mother kept running into each other in the kitchen. After a time, Mother waved her arms about and dismissed Karalee to the large dining table to put together the dressing. When Mother went to nap and give her leg a rest, Karalee was able to finish most everything. With a spurt of extra energy now that food preparation was done, Karalee took out Mother's best tablecloth and set the table. She would suffer disapproval about that tablecloth, but she used it anyway. Standing back, she enjoyed the festive ambiance.

Two hours later, satisfied, she went up to bed. Before she lay down, she stepped to the window remembering the winters before: watching for Jackson's secret sign if there should be trouble. Time had a way of slipping away. Was it two years since they'd begun? Sherman made it to the sea and the killing had stopped. Mother *would* return to her beloved Charleston whether or not the war was over. Doc said she had cheated death and Karalee sensed it was true.

The curtain fell back in place and Karalee settled her very tired body into her bed. Somehow she knew all would be well.

Sleep came quickly and was sweet. A lovely sense of giddiness lifted her from her bed before Mother could get her stiff body to cooperate. Karalee tiptoed around and checked everything. Laura would be bringing the milk from their cow over and setting it outdoors to cool. That was their family's contribution. Butter was already softening in the dish through the night, thanks to the Thompsons. There would be plenty to share today. She prepared four buttermilk pies and put them in the oven.

The celebration of Christmas in this house had died when John and then Father passed. To appear normal to others, Mother had insisted on a Christmas tree in full view from the road out front. They were not to be seen as overly-morbid, she'd said.

Having heard those words, Karalee wanted to weep...morbid no, lost and sad without her father and brother, yes.

This year was different. They were celebrating what they had died for. Freedom. A nation undivided. Free people of all colors and race. Yes, there was much to be grateful for.

A light knock at the door interrupted her thoughts. Karalee ran so Mother would not be disturbed.

"Oh, Julianne. How good to see you. Come in." Karalee hung her coat on the hall-tree Father had carved from an oak branch.

Julianne knew the household well and whispered, "I thought you could use some help this morning."

"I'll make tea and we can talk while we work," Karalee spoke with a low voice.

"Oh my," Julianne said quietly. "What a lovely table setting. I've never seen it looking so festive and beautiful."

Karalee smiled softly, "There wasn't much of a reason to decorate, until now. Come tell me how you are faring in Mr. Rutledge's grand home."

For the next hour, Julianne and Karalee sipped tea and finished last minute details. There were eggs to boil and set out. The dressing was brought in from the cold and set aside to be cooked just before the guests arrived.

"You look happy, Julianne. Are you?" Karalee stopped what she was doing and looked up.

"I am ever so happy, Karalee. All has worked for good. Mr. Rutledge was difficult at first, but I knew he would be and kept my peace, showed my faithfulness to him and did whatever he asked...except a time or two," she said shyly, eyes lowered.

"He hasn't...hasn't been untoward, has he?"

"No, I would not allow it. He hinted at it, but I immediately told him I would leave my position if he behaved in an ungentlemanly manner—word or deed."

"That was wise."

"I heard the talk." She looked up again. "I knew if I was to be a companion to him we would have to set the rules right at the start."

Karalee nodded. "I'm so glad you are safe."

"There are many people working in the house and he pays me quite well. More than we discussed at the beginning."

"Indeed?"

"I am to have three weeks every summer to do as I wish and do not have to pay board."

"How kind of him." Karalee couldn't believe she was saying that.

"He was quite disagreeable at the first," she admitted. "But he saw soon enough I would not coddle him nor put up with indecent behavior. I think he respects me."

"As he should."

They talked of other things for more than an hour and then Mother made her way out, looking quite comfortable. "Mother, I haven't seen you in a housedress and apron in ages."

"It's just an old dress. I will be changing later." She waved her arms in dismissal of the conversation and went to work. "The dressing needs to go in the stove, then the potatoes if we are to serve them done and still hot."

Julianne and Karalee looked at each other but said nothing. Mother was in charge now.

"And Karalee Elizabeth, don't think I didn't notice you used my best tablecloth."

Karalee kept her peace. Then a knock came at the front door.

"Oh who could that be? It's three hours before company is due. Don't folks have any sense?" Mother huffed.

23

Karalee rushed to the door. She saw several bodies among snow-covered green branches. They were hauling up a huge pine across the veranda. "Mother it's a Christmas tree!" Come see for yourself. Come Julianne. It's perfect."

Mother limped in, her hands twisted in her apron. "Tell them to shake off the snow and pick up the trunk. It will scratch my floor."

Karalee opened the door. Laura's father and three brothers were struggling to get it inside. They had already nailed a sturdy wood cross to the bottom of the trunk. The tree barely fit through the doublewide doorway. It was so large everyone wondered if it was *too* wide. Karalee declared it was not and moved two chairs away from the windows. Their house was large and grand with sixteen-foot ceilings. It *would* fit.

Once it was in place, they all stood back. "I declare I have never seen such a big tree," Mother exclaimed.

Karalee loved the look of awe on her mother's face. "Mama does it remind you of your childhood home? The big tree?"

"It does. Father always had the best and biggest tree we could find."

Then she remembered all she had to do. "We have cooking to do. What of decorations?" Mother asked and looked around, hands resting on her hips.

"We will be back with lots of them," Jonas said. "The girls have been stringing popcorn for two days."

"Well, be about it then." Mother shooed them off, then added, "Come hungry and not a minute before two o'clock."

Karalee shared a smile with Laura's father and then they were off.

The time passed quickly. The huge pot of potatoes boiled over twice and Mother couldn't find her best masher. They had to make do.

Soon the sausage dressing came out to cool and a second pan put in the oven. Mama was, if anything, a true Southern cook. There was enough to feed a small army and more choices than one group of people needed in a single day, but Karalee was proud of her mother, knowing she was still recovering and limping around on an injured leg.

24

Even Mother could see the joy of sharing what they had been given.

Six

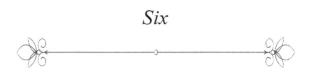

Suddenly the house exploded. Laura's family came with boxes of decorations, and a large tin pail of fresh milk now sat on the veranda, cooling and covered with a clean cloth and plate.

Karalee saw the clock was nearly ready to strike two. And Mother would not abide latecomers. It was likely Lily and Jackson had decided not to attend. Perhaps Jackson had refused.

She felt a twinge in her heart, but there was no time to worry. The two gongs of the grandfather clock declared it was time to take their places. There was an easy, quiet finding of seats. Mother had started to tell people where to sit when Karalee gave her a slight shake of her head and Mother understood.

"Sit where you like," she acquiesced.

Everyone found a place and Mother asked Laura's father to please carry in the turkey from the kitchen. When they came back, Mother found everyone standing behind a chair. Karalee smiled.

Yankees had manners, too. The look on her mother's face was priceless.

"Well, then," Mother said. "Will someone say grace?" Christmas was the one day Mother allowed grace to be said before partaking of the food.

Karalee looked to Laura's father who bowed his head. At that moment there was stomping of feet on the veranda. Mother looked up. She was not happy at the interruption.

"Karalee." She jerked her chin toward the door.

"Lily. Jackson," Karalee said softly. "Please come in."

"Please forgive us for being late," Lily apologized as her coat was hung. Karalee took Jackson's coat. He met her eyes for a second before also apologizing. "It was my doing," he stated.

Soon every chair was taken around the table.

Mother looked to Laura's father once again, her lips pressed together.

A quiet, solemn prayer of thanks was given, followed by a long silence.

Karalee saw Mother's look. Everyone was waiting for her to take her seat at the head of the table. She sat down like a queen, smoothing the back of her skirt as she lowered herself. Then there was the sound of everyone else taking their seats.

Karalee thought she could see her mother's face twitch in emotion, then recovered she squared her narrow shoulders and started the dinner. She motioned for Karalee to start passing the bowl of mashed potatoes. Usually Mother served herself first, being the lady of the house.

Suddenly the room was filled with low chatter, each one eyeing the next dish to see what was coming down the row. When every bowl had made its rounds Mama served herself. Karalee had never been more proud of her than at that moment.

God had not deserted them. After all the loss, not just for their family, but for so many others, there was redemption—if one could just hold on long enough to see it come to pass.

The dinner went on until everyone declared they could not possibly eat another bite, and then Laura's mother said it was time to decorate the tree for their host. Mother stood and said, "When the tree is done we shall have dessert." Twelve chairs scooted back and the family gathered in the parlor where the tree stood waiting. The fragrance of fresh pine permeated the entire house. Laura stayed behind to help with cleanup while her parents and brothers started the trimming.

"You may go and help them if you wish," Mama spoke to Laura kindly.

Karalee and Julianne shared a smile as Laura dashed to the parlor.

Jackson looked out of place when Lily said she would join them.

Karalee asked if he minded feeding Rosebud. She'd hardly had time. Jackson immediately grabbed his coat and she heard the back door close. The look of relief on his face was beyond price. Lily did say he was struggling. This was not the day to worry, it was a day to enjoy, Karalee reminded herself and walked back to the kitchen.

Mother set aside her towel and went out to oversee the placement of decorations on *her* tree while Karalee and Julianne prepared to wash the dishes. Mother would be back soon…she would not sit down until every last dish was accounted for, unchipped and safely back in her large glass cabinet Father had so carefully brought from Charleston when they married.

The dishes were done quickly. Julianne was efficient and excited to get in there to see the tree. Karalee wiped down the kitchen and quickly drew up the tablecloth and washed out some stains before Mother could see them.

She heard the back door open. Jackson had been out there at least an hour. Her heart beat quicker when she heard his boots stomping off snow.

He came in and asked for a cup of water.

Karalee turned to hand it to him and clapped her hand over her mouth. "What happened?"

His thick dark hair was standing at attention all over his head. His hands were dirty. "I didn't ask you to muck the stalls," she said pressing her fingers to her nose. "Better put those boots by the back door," she suggested strongly. He looked down, thinking he had cleaned them off.

"Yeah," he agreed and came back in stocking feet. "Better wash my hands, too." He shrugged.

She gave him a bar of soap and left him at the kitchen sink, with one comment over her shoulder, "Have you a comb in your pocket?" and left without waiting for an answer.

As Karalee headed toward the parlor she heard quiet talking. A soft yellow glow lit the room from the gaslights out on the street as the snow fell thick and heavy just outside the large windows. Someone had lit the candelabras around the room and the majestic tree was bedecked in all sorts of bric-a-brac. Gold and silver, red and green, turquoise and orange. White popcorn ropes looped from branch to branch around the entire tree.

It seemed no one could speak, a pity, except it was so holy a scene glowing and perfect in the quietness. The fragrance of pine brought such joy. Karalee closed her eyes and breathed it in. She felt Jackson's presence behind her. He had walked in his socks and as she turned, found him looking at the tree.

There was magic in Christmas. The silent knowing that Jesus had come and all would be well, if not now, in the times to come.

Someone started singing Silent Night. And then it was over. Karalee noticed Laura's mother began whispering to her children to get their coats.

"Dessert is next," Mother said, waving everyone back to the table.

Karalee and Julianne quickly pulled down a new batch of saucers and forks while Mother sliced the pies and cakes, then set them down the center of the table and took her place at the head. Karalee thought she might break out in laughter as Mother, queen of her house, picked up her fork and her entourage followed.

After everyone had declared they could not eat another bite, Mother stood at the door and saw each guest out. Lily and Jackson left with them. Julianne, Karalee and her mother tarried for a moment and then Mother spoke, always the practical one.

"Well, that was nice, wasn't it? It is time for bed. We have had a good day, all in all," she declared and walked slowly to her room. Karalee heard the door click.

She and her friend shared a look. "Tea?" Julianne's eyebrows lifted slightly as a soft smile lit up her face.

"Indeed," Karalee said.

The two sat in the overstuffed chairs on either side of the huge fireplace in the parlor, gazed at the tree, mesmerized, and sipped tea until their eyelids could not possibly stay open another minute.

The day was done.

Seven

New Years Day 1866

The New Year started out with as much hope as the people could pull together. They were a united nation again.

The drudgery of the worst of Michigan weather was at their doorstep. Already there were reports of a blizzard heading their way. The talk down at the General Store predicted it would be a big one. Farmers had ramped up their allotment of grain for the animals and set aside extra wood in preparation.

Mother had a few bad days following Christmas dinner. She had *done too much and aggravated her condition,* Doc said. But Laura's leg massages helped. That, and the hours she spent reading to Mother. Karalee was ever so grateful.

In mid-January an invitation came to Karalee from Julianne. She was invited to visit at Mr. Rutledge's home for a late welcome to the New Year celebration. She opened the missive and laughed aloud when she read her friend's note: "…and yes, Mr. Rutledge knows you are coming and is not in the least upset."

"What are you laughing about?" Mother called from her room.

"I have just received an invitation from Julianne to come for tea."

"What? Why would you ever enter that man's house, Karalee Elizabeth?" Mother's voice rose a notch.

"Because I want to see Julianne," she said, leaning in the doorway to Mother's room.

"That is no reason. She can come here. I don't want you going on with the likes of him. That man cannot be trusted. He has servants who will report every word you and Julianne speak."

"Would it matter, Mother? We have nothing to hide."

Mother turned on her side and pulled the coverlet over her shoulders. "There never was any dealing with you once you made up your mind," she grumped.

"I heard that, Mother."

With only three days' notice Karalee sponged her best winter dress, the color of ripe blueberries, one that required fewer crinolines and was not as wide as her hooped dresses.

The town talk had cooled to a low rumble now that time had passed since "the incident." All parties were cleared from charges with a stern warning from the judge that there had been enough damage to both sides; he did not expect to hear another word about it. Thankfully, two of the ladies who were faithful to Mother of the six at the card parties, were invited to visit. Mother felt good enough to set up the tea table in the parlor. Karalee secretly thought she really wanted to show off her beautiful Christmas tree, which she declared would stay up until the last day of January.

That was a first, for Karalee knew that Father had to nearly plead on his hands and knees to leave the tree up. *One week was enough*, Mother had always insisted. *Besides, the day has passed and no one wants the silliness of a tree twinkling in one's home for days on end.*

* * *

The day arrived for the party at the Rutledge house. Mother sulked as Karalee dressed herself and asked Laura to arrange her hair in a simple figure eight at the back of her head. Laura pinned some pretty white flowers over one ear and declared she looked beautiful. Karalee pressed scented rose water behind each ear and with a quick look in the mirror to be sure she was buttoned up, rushed downstairs at the sound of knocking. She grabbed her hooded floor-length woolen cape and opened the door.

"Jackson." Forgetting herself, she swung her gaze to look behind him as he stepped in.

"You were expecting someone?" he asked with what she thought was a deeper voice than usual, his eyes resting on hers.

"Are you ill?" She ignored his question.

He shrugged. "Getting over a chill," he admitted and took off his hat.

"Is your wound bothering you?" Karalee held his gaze to make sure she could see the truth.

31

"Some. This winter has been hard on the animals. Makes more work," he stated.

"Hmmm…it has," she agreed, setting aside her coat. He wasn't one to complain so she knew the bullet wound must still hinder him.

"You were on your way out."

"Yes." She sensed he knew where she was going. "I'm going to visit Julianne," she said firmly.

"So I hear. Do you think it wise?"

"Ah, so is this the reason for your visit?" She let a soft smile rest on her lips as she tilted her head.

When he didn't answer, Karalee gave him a look. "It's just a few blocks down the way. The carriage is coming so I won't have to walk," she explained. "I do not think it untoward to mend fences."

"As I do not." he grumped. "Keep your senses about you then," he said and punched on his hat and was out the door before she could utter a word. He didn't seem to notice she was wearing a pretty dress. Nor that she had styled her hair more elegantly.

"Well, that was strange," she muttered and heard the carriage coming down the road, which probably put him in a worse mood than if he had missed it altogether.

She slipped on her cape and carefully lifted the heavy hood over her hair, not wishing to muss it. The driver tapped at the door with his cane as she pulled on her elbow-length gloves, beneath the wide sleeves and let Mother know she was leaving.

"Who was at the door, Karalee?" she called out loudly.

"Jackson. But he is gone. I will be late this evening Mother. Don't worry."

Not a word came back. Karalee shut the door behind her and took the driver's arm.

The ride was short but glorious in the early evening sky. It was not heavy with snow up in the clouds tonight, but bright. One could enjoy the even row of snow-covered pines as they drove by, a beautiful sight.

"Karalee. It is good to have you here," Julianne said quietly as she made her way into the entrance hall. Live green ferns in large Italian clay pots adorned the walls on either side with a row of tables and mirrors leading the way. The butler took her wrap and disappeared into a side room.

"We have many guests tonight. It seems there is a secret in the works. Some very official people are here." Julianne gave her a look.

"Oh, it's nice to be among people. I can feel the excitement." She smiled at Julianne. "You must tell me all."

Julianne ignored her last comment, and then said longingly, "Blue looks so lovely with your skin."

"Thank you, but you have such white skin, as most of the ladies desire," Karalee bemoaned and gave her a look. She hated her darker tone. Father had Italian blood and she always felt like the white porcelain skin men admired would never be hers. She shrugged and blamed it on the fact she did spend a bit too much time outdoors in the sun.

"Perhaps the ladies, but not all of the men," Julianne said with a knowing grin.

Julianne's easy smile lifted her spirit and Karalee made a tease of her own. "Is there the prospect of an engagement announcement this evening, as well?" Karalee stopped, pressed her hands together at her waist and waited for an answer,

"There may be but I will say no more."

"Oh, do tell." Karalee felt a delicious wave wash over her. She was in the mood for some newsy tidbit. Something that would liven up the long winter days. And, if time allowed, she needed some woman-to-woman talk. Jackson had cooled his intentions and she was at a loss as to why.

"I cannot tell. But there is something big in the air," she taunted. "I am free to roam about tonight with Mr. Rutledge's full support. He said he is to be quite busy. And I am to spread good rumors about him." She gave Karalee a look.

"As long as they are true."

"Well, they would not be rumors then," she shot back.

"You have adapted quite well to the way of things, it seems."

"I have learned well how to present myself…and my employer," she agreed.

The buzz of well-dressed ladies and gentlemen filled the large ballroom. Tables laid out in a half circle invited guests to help themselves to the savories and pastries. Dozens of candles danced along the wall, reflecting off the huge chandelier in the middle of the room, sending light bouncing from every corner. The aromas coming from the cook's room reminded Karalee she'd hardly eaten all day. A sit-down dinner around the huge twenty-four seat table was slated for an eight o'clock serve. Karalee had overheard that from one of the footmen.

Julianne led her to a small room. They slipped through the door and shut it behind them.

"A library?" Karalee ran her fingers across the books on the shelves. "Quite studious from the titles."

"Very. It seems one of Mr. Rutledge's weaknesses is that he is a slow reader, so he fills his shelves with books that would impress any visitor."

Karalee looked up. Was Julianne making a mockery of her employer or just joking?

"You do not laugh. So then it is true?" Karalee spoke softly.

"Perhaps I should not have spoken," she said quickly, her brown eyes large.

"If it is thus, then it is thus. I do not judge," Karalee said formally. "For I would have no idea whether these books were full of grand ideas or recipes for evening suppers."

"I do love our visits, Karalee. You lift me up. You have not a single worry what others think. I wish I were more like you."

"On the contrary, my dear friend, you must not wish yourself like me. For you see, I have other maladies that are not so sweet as your kind and generous nature, most especially to someone who must be very difficult to please." She made known her point.

"He was at first, but I was firm."

"There, you see!"

"I knew that if I were not, I would go rushing down the street in a fit of tears, never to show my face around this town again. I have no husband and no parents. I must make my own way," Julianne said.

"Indeed you must," Karalee said softly as she picked up one of the books and thumbed through it, then closed it and put it back. "Way above *my* head," she declared, to which Julianne laughed.

"I have not had time to look at one of them."

"He keeps you quite busy then?"

"Oh yes, but I would have it no other way. He is demanding, but when he steps out of line I give him a certain look and he acts like he has not seen it, but adjusts his temper ever so slightly a few moments later."

"You have bewitched him," Karalee laughed.

"I doubt that will ever be the matter," she said and they heard the dinner gong.

Julianne smoothed her skirt and rushed to the door. "He abhors lateness. I must be at my station," she said and hurried out. Karalee followed in her wake, for her friend was sailing down the gilded hallway, her skirts swinging like a ringing bell. She, on the other hand, had no need to hurry. It felt good to be among people and she looked forward to an elegant meal. She and Mother had lost their desire to make big meals or fanciful desserts for just the two of them.

Truth was, she missed the work she and Jackson had been doing. And now that she had been put aside, their relationship seemed to cool. Thinking thus, she made it a point to be a respectable guest and talk to others. She and Mother would soon be leaving the area, which allowed a bit of freedom to breathe. Heaven knows what some might think. Mother having shot Mr. Rutledge and him returning the favor. Suddenly a feeling of de-ja-vu came over her. Maybe it had been unwise for her to come. Yet no one seemed to stare or pass by whispering behind their hand.

Her thoughts were interrupted when she heard the call for couples to present themselves and be announced: very formal gathering, indeed. It seemed Julianne had disappeared. She looked around and as she did, Mr. Rutledge caught her eye. It was the first they had seen each other since the incident.

He nodded slightly and she returned the gesture in kind. He was coming her way in his rather elegant wheeled conveyance. "Miss Williams, we meet under very different circumstances, do we not?" he asked and pulled a cigar from his mouth.

"As you see," she said smiling. "Are you faring well then?" she inquired and could have bit her tongue off.

"As well as can be expected," he admitted and took another puff. Smoke meandered upward and she pressed her hands to her cheeks instead of her nose.

"I remember you dislike the fragrance of cigars."

She chose to acknowledge with a smile and let it go. He was acting more gentlemanly these days and she had no quarrel with him.

35

He could have, with his round of lawyers, filed charges against Mother since she fired at him first and proved he was only protecting himself.

Tonight she was especially happy she was free of him and made small conversation. "It seems like a very lively group this evening," she said looking around.

"Indeed it is," he said and was called away by a footman.

Moments later she heard a deep voice directly over her shoulder. "A lady without a gentleman to escort her to dinner?"

Karalee turned and found herself looking at a man's uniform. She quickly turned her eyes upward and saw a nice face, a full foot taller than herself.

"As you see," she said kindly.

"We will introduce ourselves, since the need is at hand. "I am Sergeant John Harris Swift, Michigan, 7th Calvary, and I have the pleasure of meeting . . . ?"

"Miss Karalee Williams," she said simply, to which he bowed slightly, his Union uniform indicating he was an officer. She immediately wondered why a Union officer was in Mr. Rutledge's house. Their host was a born and bred Southern gentleman.

"Miss Williams, will you do me the honor of letting me escort you?" He bowed slightly.

"Yes you may," she answered using her formal voice and before she knew it they were seated side-by-side at the long table.

Julianne was already seated near the head of the table, in fact to Mr. Rutledge's immediate right. A huge smile rested on her face as Karalee realized Julianne was gazing at the gentleman sitting next to her. Had she arranged this soldier's escort?

Mr. Rutledge tapped his knife on a glass, formally beginning the proceedings. Since he could not stand, he spoke from his chair and everyone stood.

He greeted his guests, thanked them for their presence and looked around the room then lifted his goblet high. There was a great clinking of glass-to-glass in the room and low chatter before everyone sat down.

Karalee was still unaware of the exact reason for the "celebration." And when she thought of it...why *she* was here at all.

After the formal serving, eating and proper etiquette—talking first with the guest on the left, which happened to be a debonair older gentleman with white hair and well-kept beard, then the officer on the right—she was quite tired. She remembered why formal occasions were not her forte.

After a time, glass was tapped, louder this time as conversation was still buzzing around the table. Everyone stood. Mr. Rutledge said he preferred to speak eye to eye and asked his guests to sit down. There followed a bit of good-natured laughter.

"It is my pleasure to announce that I have been nominated for Governor of the State of Michigan for the next election. And I have accepted that nomination."

A loud round of applause went around the table. And much congratulating and raising of glasses.

When the noise died down, while waiting for the next course, Sergeant Swift leaned over and said, "Jasper and I played together as young boys. Our parents were neighbors. I moved up here long ago, but I sense our Mr. Rutledge wanted to be sure his Northern counterparts did not still think of him as a Confederate. It would ruin his chances at the voting polls up here in Yankee country."

Appalled at first, Karalee chanced a gaze his way and saw a pair of green eyes dancing. "Oh how informative," she said, and pressed two fingers to her lips. His deep voice was pleasant next to her ear.

"I thought you might think so," Miss Williams.

Thankfully, she managed to get through the next two courses. Sergeant Swift was not only handsome, but very entertaining.

Soon the guests were mingling in smaller groups, talking about the announcement. The ladies gathered in the front parlor, which Karalee noted was at least double in size to their already large one, and the men were smoking cigars and sipping sherry in a room down the wide hall. Mr. Rutledge *did* know how to entertain and his home was one of the grandest in the county.

But Karalee could not help thinking if the public knew of his marital indiscretions he would be laughed out of the race by the good people in his own county, let alone the entire State of Michigan. But, then again, politics did have its gaggle of evil men in every generation. Be it far from her to judge. Everyone had their skeletons.

She was musing when Julianne came and stood nearby. "So there you have it," she whispered. "The word is out."

"And of course, you already knew."

"Since I am his caretaker, I heard enough to know, but I did my duty and did not tell a soul."

"It was to your honor," Karalee said truthfully. "But now that it is known, what have you to say about it?"

She saw Julianne look around. "Shall we retire to the library and leave the guests to their musings?"

"Yes. It seems Sergeant Swift is already surrounded by ladies." She smiled.

Slowly, Julianne disengaged herself from a conversation and Karalee followed her to the library where the servants brought tea at Julianne's request.

"You are now in the midst of a huge change," Karalee warned her. "The times are not pleasant and soon you will be surrounded by political, dare I say, goons?"

"Yes. But Father taught me well! *Stand your ground. Make your point. And close your mouth.*" Julianne delivered her own speech.

Karalee laughed aloud. "Very good advice indeed. I think you shall do just fine as your governor-elect's sidekick."

"Sidekick?" Now Julianne was laughing. "I should say I am his caretaker-become-secretary as much as anything."

"You do your job well. I am so happy for you, my friend," Karalee said.

"Oh, look, now you have unnerved me."

"Truly, you have cared for your mother, lost your beloved father and here you are in the house of a Governor-hopeful. I should say you are quite the strong woman," Karalee reminded her.

Julianne waved off her comment. "Let's have tea. I want nothing more, now that the announcement is out, than to sit here and enjoy this evening. Mr. Rutledge has his men to keep him occupied tonight. They are already discussing plans, I daresay. They have been holed up in his office for nearly two weeks."

"So long?"

"Politics. It is a process that must be carefully thought out," She shrugged. "Sugar?"

"Yes, thank you."

The evening passed in quiet conversation, the only interruptions as servants came with more tea. "I have so enjoyed having time to chat with you, my dear friend. I've missed our visits, Karalee. And I want to thank you for taking me in after Mother passed and for helping me through the loss of a young man I thought would sweep me away. Alas, I find myself here, and stronger because of it. I have found purpose."

Karalee stood. "I must be getting back to Mother. I hope you see that you were made for this work, Julianne, and I am proud to know you. "

The women exchanged a few last words, and then Julianne reached for the cord to ring for a driver.

The short ride home was freezing. Karalee walked through the front door, the fragrance of fresh pine greeting her once again. She hung her wrap, shook the snow off her boots and set them aside. Mother was asleep, her door shut, a sign she did not want to be disturbed.

She slipped up the stairs, wrote in her journal, and crawled into a very warm bed after adding extra logs to the fires below.

Thankful she was free of Mr. Rutledge and glad all was well, she thought about Jackson and knew he had nothing to worry about. The evening had been uneventful.

Eight

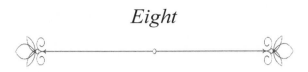

Jackson paced the floor all evening. How could Karalee forget all that Rutledge had done? The man was not to be trusted. Did she have feelings for him perhaps? He thought she had more sense than to visit his house again.

A stop at Lily's on the way back from the unplanned visit to Karalee's had put him in a bad mood. Even his sister said people should be forgiven if they are trying to right their wrongs. And it sounded as though she thought Rutledge was a changed man.

Lily explained to her brother that she had heard through the incessant chatter of the ladies in town that he had turned a corner after his follies had found him out, and was now running for Governor.

"Like running for Governor will change a man's heart," Jackson grumped aloud. Women were so susceptible. He headed home.

Twice he had the strongest desire to go over and inform Mrs. Williams he was going to be out back mucking Rosebud's stall and hang around until Karalee arrived home safely. And twice he had managed to force himself not to go.

Frustrated, he pulled the big tin tub into the kitchen, warmed water and took a long, hot bath. Besides, Karalee and her Mother would be going to Charleston. Another hindrance. They would be gone for months, maybe forever. Karalee said she wanted to come back to her birthplace, but Jackson knew her Mother held a strong influence over her daughter.

What then? Later, tossing in bed, he formed two plans: one with Karalee, one without. If he chose to win her over he would have to tell her something about himself that would likely change the way she thought of him. If he let her go, she could find someone more worthy of her.

There was one thing he would *not* do: make her life miserable. She had almost fallen for Rutledge's fast talk. Jackson would have preferred she accepted his own offer of marriage rather than one from the man who already had two wives. But she had refused his offer...not once, but twice.

God forbid, he would ever mess up her life. Karalee was a good woman, had put up with his lack of kindness while they worked together. He had made it a point not to allow anything to come between him and his work. Not even her.

Then she had stolen his heart when she fell apart, not knowing how to handle someone like Rutledge. She was strong but naïve at the same time.

What he knew of the world, he could see she was too vulnerable. He had finally found a reason to stop allowing her to help and when he thought of it, realized he had wanted her just to be a woman, not his partner, which required him to be crushingly hard on her and responsible for her safety. Things had gotten out of hand and he had fallen victim to those sad, dark eyes when she felt like she had failed him.

He had wanted to take her in his arms and protect her—from dishonest men, from the hatefulness and evil in the world—but refrained. Then he had broken his own rule, had held her in his arms and too quickly declared his love for her.

Jackson turned and punched his pillow. He had made a mess of things.

His thoughts ran to the fact that if she never knew his past, she would not have to forgive him. He could let her go. She could seek another man, a more truthful, kinder one.

Those thoughts kept him awake far into the night.

* * *

Next thing he knew, someone was pounding at his door. He untangled himself from the covers, stood to the side of the window, peeked through the curtain and groaned.

"What is *he* doing here?" he grumped, quickly pulled on his undershirt and trousers, then jerked the suspenders over his shoulders. But if he was here, was Sadie? No, she would never come here. No one knew about Sadie, except Lily.

He knew the man by name and had seen him once from a picture. Jackson had hired a man to find her and report back to let him know if Sadie was all right. His stomach twisted into a knot as he made his way to the door. With a quick movement he finger-brushed his hair to smooth out the tangles and opened it.

"Jackson Woodridge?"

"Yep." He looked over the man's shoulder—there was only one horse.

"I'm Ely Emery."

"Yes." He pretended not to know him. "What is your business?"

"I married Sadie Sanderson."

"And?" Jackson felt a stab of pain at the man's words.

"I am here to ask if you know you have a child?"

"What?" Jackson glared at him. "I have no child." He started to close the door.

Mr. Emery pressed his foot to the door. "My wife, as you know, was Sadie Sanderson before I married her. We have a son, or I thought he was my son."

Jackson frowned. "What is that to me?"

"On her deathbed, she confessed the child was not mine, but yours."

"Deathbed?" Jackson felt his entire body stiffen.

"Not a month ago."

"You must be mistaken."

"Then you deny you knew her?"

"I do not deny that." Jackson gave him a look.

"The child I thought was mine is yours. I am bringing him back to you. It was her last request."

The words lay thick in the air. Jackson swallowed hard, looked out over the man's head and tried to process what he was saying. Was he lying? He had a son?

"How can you know he's mine?"

"I came to see for myself. The child looks nothing like me. He is *your* son. I know now what she said was true."

Jackson felt the man's pain as he stood there waiting. "Wouldn't the child prefer to stay with you? He does not know me."

"She told the boy, too."

42

Jackson's head fell low between his shoulders and he felt his stomach lurch. When he had gathered his wits, he looked up and said, "Go back home. Tell the boy to stay where he's at. I'm unmarried and it would not be good for him to be without a mother." Sweet Sadie was dead. And so young. An instant sense of guilt passed over him like a dark cloud.

"The boy is eight," Ely said firmly. "Would that be the right time?"

"Mr. Emery, I will answer no more questions. As you can imagine, I need time to think. Give me your address and I will write."

"I am not leaving until I have an answer. The boy is beside himself with grief over losing his mother, and now he knows I am not his father. I…I have loved the boy like my own son."

Jackson looked down as the man's eyes went soft with grief.

"But the truth is the truth. I would not deny her request."

"You can't just come and leave him here. Give me your address and I *will* write," he stated firmly.

"And if you don't, I'll bring him anyway. The deed is done. The boy has a right to know his own father. There can be no turning back. It was her request. I will fulfill it if I can. You've got two months, Woodridge. You can reach me at the post office in Schoolcraft."

Jackson nodded and noted the way he spoke of Sadie. He was fulfilling her wishes even though it was killing him.

With that, Ely Emery covered his head with his hat, walked slowly back to his horse and mounted. Jackson watched the snow kick up behind him as he left.

He shut the door against the cold, not realizing he was freezing. He hadn't even asked the man if he wanted to come inside and get warm. It seemed like their conversation lasted forever, when in reality he was probably there no longer than three minutes…enough time to change his whole life. And Ely Emory's. He'd lost his wife and now his son.

Sadie was dead. Jackson fell down in a chair, elbows on his knees, hands kneading through his hair first, then across his face over and over again. He stared at the floor as he remembered her: young, sweet and faithful, while he had been none of those things.

After a time, he wept. For her, for the boy, for Ely Emory and yes, for himself. What was he supposed to do now?

43

Nine

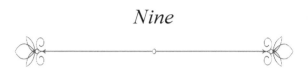

After a while, Jackson forced himself to get up and add logs to the fire, pull on his boots and do the chores. It kept his mind from going crazy. He had a son? He worked outside chopping wood with a vengeance and cleaned out the barn until dark.

All the stuff of his ugly past, which he had worked hard to leave behind, came flying back like black crows darkening the sky. They hung over him, thick and foreboding. He could think of nothing else. Memories, one at a time, swooped down: Sadie's long blond hair, soft skin and beautiful blue eyes. Her kind and sweet ways. She had loved him and he had never been the man she deserved. He had gone as far as he could abide, until finally he had pushed her away. And the next thing he knew, she was married. He was glad. He would never be good enough for her and so he made sure she would be free of him. He had walked away and thought it was all behind him.

By evening Jackson was so tired of thinking, he went to bed without dinner.

He didn't even know the boy's name.

The next day, after a sleepless night, Jackson finished chores early, saddled up Stockton and headed down to Lily's place. She would have to hear all the sordid details. She knew about Sadie, but it was going to be hard to tell her about the boy.

There was no going around it. He had made choices and now they were back to remind him of his failures. Best to get it done and over with. Lily would help him figure this out.

He grabbed a day-old biscuit, downed it with two cups of boiling coffee, pulled on his long overcoat, and settled his hat low over his face against the blowing snow.

He had hardly realized the sun was just coming up over the horizon, but it couldn't be helped. "We've got work to do, Stock." He patted his mount and gave him a handful of oats, broke the ice off the top of a water bucket and set it nearby. He knocked hard on Lily's door.

His sister peeked out the window and was yawning as she pulled her heavy wrapper around her gown.

"Gotta talk, sis," he said and stomped off his boots. He left them by the front door, tossed his coat over the nail then his hat and gloves.

"What's wrong?" Lily said as she hurried to shut the door against the blowing snow.

Jackson sat down in the nearest chair and looked up.

"I'll get coffee," she said, heart beating fast.

He waved his hand. "I just had two cups. Coffee can't fix this mess, sis," he said hearing the grim tone of his own voice.

Lily poured a cup of tea for herself. Anytime he called her sis, there was a heart to heart talk coming. Immediately, she thought it was about Karalee. She said a prayer and took her time settling herself on the settee across from her brother.

Half her tea was gone by the time he got the nerve to speak up. She wished it wasn't so hard for him to communicate, but she knew why, so she waited.

He took a deep breath, looked up.

Lily's heart went out to him. He hadn't slept, hadn't shaved. She knew her brother. This was something big. She steeled her heart and hoped he wasn't leaving again.

"I had a visitor yesterday. Ely Emory," he stated and locked eyes with her.

Lily waited, saying nothing. She knew who Ely Emory was.

"Sadie passed."

At the news, Lily pressed her fingers to her lips. "Sadie?" She made sure she heard right.

"Yeah, he came to tell me."

"Jackson, I'm so sorry. What happened?"

"He didn't say. I guess I didn't think to ask."

She nodded.

"There's more, Lily. She had a son. He's eight years old."

"Eight?" Lily said. "So young to be without his mother."

He hated the hurt in Lily's voice.

"I'm so sorry for both of them, Ely and his son," she said softly.

"The boy's not his son."

Lily looked at him.

"He's my son."

"But..." she started to speak and stopped.

"She confessed to her husband on her death bed that the boy was not his, but mine."

Lily felt water gathering in her eyes and pinched the bridge of her nose, willing herself not to cry.

"Tell me all," she said with a weak voice. Her brother's countenance nearly undid her. She had seen Jackson at his lowest and this was right up there at the top.

"You know I pushed her away. I knew I wouldn't make a good husband, not with my temper. But she stayed with me. She even..." He hung his head.

Lily waited, tears flowing down her face. It was all coming up again. The past. Father and his temper, the way he treated Mama.

To the world their family had looked like the typical happy family, especially since they owned the largest land parcel in the county. Everyone thought they were wealthy. Maybe in land they were, but as far as a loving family, they were sorely lacking.

Their father was known to be an honest man in his dealings, but he had a low threshold for anyone who crossed him at home. And when he had threatened to push Mama and started taking his anger out on her, thirteen-year-old Jackson stepped in. And from that day forward, their father turned his anger on his son.

Jackson couldn't do anything right. And even if he did, father criticized it. Mama tried to defend him, but that made things worse for her. Finally at sixteen Jackson rode his horse out of town and was gone for two years. Father talked of his "blackened" son, ruining his standing in the town by leaving a "good home" and his inheritance. Nothing was ever father's fault.

Lily fared well, because Father had favored her. And she had hated it. Mama and Jackson could never please him. Lily was not yet eighteen when he fell over dead in the barn one day. Mama died the following year. Mama, with all the hurt she had suffered in his wake, missed him and could not be consoled.

Lily finally found Jackson living with Mama's brother in Ohio, working on their farm. When she told Jackson that our father had died he refused to come back for the funeral. When Mama died, Jackson came home. He soon learned his own father had removed his son's name from the deed, proving that his son was a no-good. Lily got the farm and all the land.

After Jackson came back from Ohio, Lily signed the farm over to him and kept the small house next door. There was no way she could handle the place alone. She took the role of younger sister and gave Jackson his rightful inheritance.

* * *

Sadie Sanderson was their schoolmate. She had loved Jackson secretly since the fourth level. Sadie had waited nearly her entire life for him. While he was gone she had grown up. She was two years behind him in school. Lily remembered her well. She was sweet, from a poor but good family, and Lily could see the love she had for her brother.

Jackson was angry, drank too much and was generally a nuisance. Sadie's parents went to church but Jackson refused to go. He hated all the looks he got and didn't like answering questions from the church people who were too nosy: Why had he left? Wasn't he drinking a bit too much? . . . this from the ladies in town. Father didn't believe in going to church. Said it was a weakness for a man to have to sit on a pew when so much work had to be done.

Mama had gone to Sunday services when she could, but he had broken her down until she finally quit going. It was easier to stay home and work than to see his angry glare as they rode off.

Sadie's father, Mr. Sanderson, had been good to her brother, but after a few times seeing Jackson's temper was like his father's, he felt his daughter was better off waiting for him to get hold of himself. He was an angry young man. Then when he came drunk to pick up Sadie one day, her father put a stop to their visits.

Lily, when she thought back, felt like Jackson created the situation so Mr. Sanderson would throw him out, because for all the world, Lily knew Jackson had loved Sadie more than his own life. But he was afraid he would turn out like our father and finally pushed her away.

Lily forced herself to stop remembering.

"But he raised the boy. Why would he give him up?"

47

"Sadie told the boy the truth before she died. And the boy wants to come here."

"Oh, Jackson." She pressed her hands together in her lap. "Doesn't Ely want him?"

"Not if the boy wants to come here. Ely said he would do as Sadie asked and leave it up to the boy," he said and looked up.

"What is his name?" Lily asked softly.

She saw his dark eyes and the film of water that formed over them. "I didn't even ask," he said and lowered his head.

She swiped angrily at her tears, but said nothing until she could get herself under control. Those two minutes were the hardest silence she'd had to endure.

"You know God is in this somewhere, right?" she asked, her voice wavering.

"Truth is, Lily. I *don't* know." He stood and paced.

"It's all right. I heard what you said, I know how things were, Jackson, and I somehow feel it will all turn out if we keep our senses about us." She could hardly believe the words she had just said. But she did believe them. "Wait and see. We'll work on this."

Jackson couldn't see things the way his sister did. If it wasn't black and white, hard-labor related, or something tangible he could touch or fix, he wasn't sure about it. He had long ago learned to push his feelings down, deep down inside.

"That's why I came here first thing."

"I'm glad you did. You have two months to write back?"

"Yep, that's what he said.

"Okay, let's think about this." She stood. "Breakfast?"

Jackson looked at her. Lily could see relief in his face.

When he nodded she set to work. Nothing like cooking to take a man's mind off his troubles. For her part, she was glad to just stand up and be busy herself. It was like pulling the heaviness off her chest and throwing it aside. She could breathe again.

"I'll get some wood chopped. You're low."

"Thanks," she said, glad to see him working. "Extra, if you don't mind. I don't relish having to go out there and drag it up to the porch."

Jackson walked out the door and her heart slowed. "Jackson has a son." She whispered into the air.

Ten

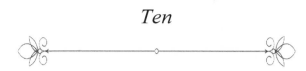

Three weeks passed. Karalee wondered why Jackson had not come around. Maybe he was miffed at her attendance at Mr. Rutledge's or perhaps that the man had announced he was running for Governor, especially since Jackson knew so much of his sordid past.

Karalee felt the fact that he had slowly been disengaging with her was also a sign. With her and Mother going south as soon as they could manage, she would be gone. It would give her time to think.

There was one thing she wanted: a man who was like her Father. And if that meant waiting, then she would wait. Jackson had been more moody the few times she saw him. At first she had accounted it to his injuries. It was hard to keep a man down when he needed to heal. Perhaps he had done too much and was paying for it. She was not the type of woman to go running after a man, especially if he didn't really want her. But that kiss they shared . . . lingered in her mind. That had been real. What had changed?

Karalee forced herself to quit guessing about what was going to happen; there was plenty to do.

Today was the second week of February. If things worked out like the Union newspapers said, she and Mother would be able to catch a train from Chicago. Except they had gotten word, after much speculation, that they would have to take a stagecoach at the end of the trip because many rail lines had been destroyed in Charleston and surrounding areas.

That did not stop Mama from making her plans. Her best dishes were packed in sawdust, three trunks of them. And Mama insisted that they be sent on ahead. Who in the world was going to load those trunks up and take them to the train? Not to mention, who might be there to receive them if they *did* arrive safely. Karalee's nerves were frazzled and at the back of her mind, she wondered about Jackson.

"Karalee, I need help with my bath," Mother called.

"I'll be right there." Karalee dusted off her hands, in the midst of cleaning Mama's knickknacks one by one and wrapping them in linens.

"Laura's coming soon. Can you wait for her? I'm very dusty at the moment." Karalee stood in her mother's bedroom doorway.

Mother answered stiffly, but acquiesced.

"I've almost got the shelf cleared and we have another trunk, albeit a smaller one than the last three. Mother, do you know how much it's going to cost to ship these down?"

Mother waved away the concern of cost, which just caused another thought to race through Karalee's mind. "Do you know if Grandaddy and Granmama are back there yet?"

"Of course they cannot travel, thanks to those Yankees burning everything on the way to the sea! Blast Sherman. The rail lines are still not repaired."

Karalee stood in the doorway one second longer and shook her head. What could she say? She went back to work and half an hour later heard Laura knock and come through the door.

"Good morning, Karalee," she said brightly. "It looks like you've been busy."

"Very." Karalee smiled at Laura's soft voice and pondered her ability to handle Mother…this not for the first time. "She would like a bath this morning."

"I'll see to it. Then perhaps, if she is up to it, we can work on some embroidering. Your mother is going to teach me."

"What a good idea, Laura. Mother's work is beautiful as I'm sure you've noticed."

"Indeed I have and I'm afraid my mother never has time to embroider. She is too busy mending." Laura laughed lightly.

Karalee stopped dusting to watch her walk away. Laura knew what she wanted to do. There was always a place for every person in the world. She was just wishing she knew where her place was. Waxing dull in her thinking, she stepped out the front door, brushed out her skirts, sending dust flying, then went to the kitchen for a cup of tea, and back to work.

Late in the afternoon, she walked out to talk to Rosebud and took her for a short ride. The skies were blue and the sun was bright. Snow had melted off and the ground was mushy, but she needed a long, slow ride. Mother's voice complaining about every little thing to Laura had worn her down. Today she donned Father's gloves. They had been sitting on the bench in the stalls where he had left them. Karalee needed him near today. And she missed John so badly—if she could only talk to him. Mostly her thoughts went to days past and she felt deep inside Jackson was about to join that rank: her past.

What had she done? she wondered as Rosebud, happy to be out and about, plodded along. Karalee noted her skirts were already muddied and heavy around her legs. There was no way to avoid puddles and in fact, Rosebud seemed to enjoy mucking through them. She smiled and was savoring the feeling of sun on her face, when she heard a wagon coming. It was still around the corner, but she knew that rattle. Jackson.

Shuttering her emotions, she smoothed the loose strands of hair around her ears. It was all she had time to do before they came face to face in the middle of the road.

He pulled his team to a stop. Rosebud whinnied and her nostrils blew out at the sight of Jackson.

"Hey Rosebud, she's got you out for a walk."

It stung that he greeted her horse before he gave his attention to her.

"Karalee." He tipped his hat.

Was that all he had to say? "Jackson."

"I'm on my way to town."

She felt his gaze linger as he said the words. It was a longing gaze. But she truly didn't know what to do. They were no longer working together and heaven forbid that he come calling on her. She decided right then that she would not force any man to court her. If he didn't want to be around, then she was fine with that. Thinking thus, she said, "Well, I'd better let you get to it." She lifted her chin and sent Rosebud forward with a squeeze to her flanks

Jackson lifted his hat and slapped the reins.

Karalee knew he was not the same man. Something had changed but she knew not what it was. Perhaps God thought it best. He sure must have, because she was headed to Charleston.

She decided to attend church this next Sunday. She missed the pastor's uplifting words. And if truth were told, she needed some good preaching these days.

Eleven

March came roaring in with another blizzard. Karalee was tiring of the daily snow. Mother was anxious to go, especially since more than half the house had been packed up. She had hired several young men from the church to move the trunks. Father's office trunk went out to the stable, all of Mother's went on a wagon and then to the train depot.

Money was dwindling. Mother never thought about the cost it would take to move everything she had accumulated. Karalee could only hope that once they arrived in Charleston, there would be someone there to take care of her. Their funds were drawing to a dangerous low. Karalee dreaded even bringing up the topic of money. Father had warned her early on that Mother thought they would, as a matter of course, never run out of it.

To that end, the first thing she did was remember what the pastor said, "Pray first, act later."

* * *

On the last day of March, early in the morning and after much thought given to setting out her idea, Karalee announced at breakfast, "Mother I think we need to sell the house."

"Whatever for?" She looked over her teacup. "Where would you live? I know you don't plan on staying with your mother, Karalee. Have you no sense?"

"Mother as you see, I am not married. A single woman living in this huge house?"

"You could have taken my advice and groomed yourself for a suitable marriage, Karalee Elizabeth."

Karalee hated the whine in Mother's voice and as usual felt like a scolded child. She nearly blurted out words she would no doubt regret later. It was no use sharing even a tiny piece of her heart with Mother.

"That boy Jackson didn't turn out to be the man you thought, did he? I see he has not called on you in weeks, which to my way of thinking, serves you right. He's nothing but a dusty farmer and your life would be mucking around stalls all day, much like you do for your... your horse out there, riding off down the road all the time like a heathen. It's no wonder a respectable man will not even consider you for a wife."

Karalee felt her insides burn with anger. She rose and said smartly, "You know Mother, I think you're right. I need some good company today. Rosebud will do just fine." And with that, she smacked her teacup down on the table and went upstairs to her room.

After writing in her journal, burning the pencil across the paper, she dressed in heavy clothing and went out to the barn. "Rosebud, you and I are going for a ride." Her mount knew they were going out and became quite anxious to be about it.

"Come on, girl. We're going to the woods today and muck around, climb that tree, just for the fun of it and see if Jackson has left any secret notes."

Suddenly, tears began to fall. Angry tears. Hurt tears. But, for all the wrong reasons, she *had* to check that tree. Jackson wasn't one to communicate freely. She knew that much about him. Maybe, just maybe. She knew it was desperation. But Karalee didn't care at the moment. If the door was shut, then it was shut. But if there was a chance...she was going to take it.

The weather proved to be quite good. It seemed there would be an early spring. April was here, and the hope of green buds on the thickly wooded trees would soon be a reality in Michigan as was the fact she was leaving the state she was born in.

Karalee took the back roads and mucked her way through the trees until she came to the *one*.

Wrapping Rosebud's reins around a bush, she looked at the tree, still bare from the long winter, yet strong and tall. The clouds above were fluffy against the bright blue sky. The smell of dirt freshened by snow then sun, wafted up. The forest was see-through right now, whereas all summer she had been hidden by the lush leaves and bushes. She looked around. The place was secret. Only she and Lily

53

and Jackson knew about it and for certain, she didn't want to expose their hiding place.

Karalee lent her ear, looked around again, and quickly climbed the tree. Thankfully, she had on her split skirt riding gear today. She reached for the box. It was still there, damp, a little moldy but there. She shook it and opened carefully. Empty. Slowly she closed it and placed it safely where it belonged and climbed down.

"Rosebud, it looks like my work is finished here in Michigan. Perhaps I should not come back." They rode through the woods, Karalee feeling free, yet sad. She had asked God for a sign and guessed this must be it.

The rest of the ride was about making her next plan. Father, John, and one day Mother would be gone. Maybe her mother had been right. She should have been more feminine, attended the teas, and put up with the silliness of a woman seeking a man to provide for her in exchange for a wife.

Dreadful. All dreadful. She wanted a marriage, just not like the ones she saw in her circle. She wanted someone to know her. To love her for the good she had in her and yes, she wanted someone to love her even when she wasn't perfect. Was it too much to ask? Thus far, her only experience with anything close to love was Jackson and she had failed at that. Her Mother's words kept pounding in her ears. How foolish was she to lose the young years when, whatever beauty she may possess was at its zenith, she could've grabbed some man and married him...because she was desperate?

Suddenly, it occurred to her. She was *not* her Mother. She was a different person who wanted different things. Confidence welled up in her, fighting the need to be accepted. She had to live the way her heart knew it must.

"Come on, Rosebud. Let's head back. It will be what it will be. But I'll not go down without a fight."

Riding cleared her head, praying cleared her conscience. God had made her and He was the only one who knew what she was meant to do. No one else. Not even Mother.

Back at the house, which was empty of most of the doo-dads and dishes, she wondered how to spend the afternoon. Ah... the smokehouse was still full. Something would have to be done with all the meat the Thompsons had left. Mother and Karalee were now rich in food, but low in cash. She had an idea. Start helping others with the meat. In the space of two months she could find others who needed it. None would go to waste. She would see to that. Armed with a new purpose, Karalee stepped up to the back door, scraped her booted feet on the iron blade and then knocked off the mud. She left her boots at the door on the rug and went inside and up the stairs.

She pulled off her split skirt and laid it on the wood floor carefully. Clumps of mud were already falling off it. Laughing, she put herself in her sturdiest work dress, picked up the muddy skirt, carried it outdoors and shook it out, then put it over a bush to dry out completely.

Mother would hate that the neighbors might see it, but she rarely came outside, so perhaps she wouldn't notice.

Karalee was tired of what the neighbors might think.

That done, she came back inside and busied herself with the topmost part of the house, the attic. She had left this for last, knowing the mementos that meant the most to her would be up there. Indeed they were, for as she climbed up the short ladder into the third floor parapet, she laid eyes on a rocking horse, made by her father, first for John and then for her. Memories flooded her mind immediately. Mother may not want it, but Karalee would not part with it. It was one tangible memory that would remain with her. She wanted her children, if ever there were any, to ride this horse.

She touched it. Dust flew from the yarn mane Father had so carefully cut and braided to look real. She'd heard the story from him. He'd made it for John when the news first came that he was due to join the family. *And later for you*, he had added, his brown eyes letting her know he welcomed his children.

Karalee couldn't stop weeping as she went from item to item. Their cradle. Father had made that, too...a small child's chair to sit at the table... several carved wooden toys, one of them a train, and one a bird. Then she came upon a set of framed pictures, leaning against a wall with a blanket covering them. She slipped off the blanket and set each picture under the low eave against the wall. Mother and Father's wedding photo. She barely remembered it. Why had Mama stuck it up here? She studied it. Mother was the epitome of beautiful and Father was so very handsome in his Citadel uniform. Mother—her striking black hair and light eyes, her slender waist, her stunning wedding dress — warranted royalty status. Their smiles.

Her delicate mother. Karalee knew she was a disappointment to her, having father's dark eyes and skin. John had been a duplicate of his father, except for his coloring. He had the black hair and blue eyes of his mother, but his father's tall, strong body. Karalee sobbed. John's beautiful heart and body ravaged. And it was because of Mother. Hatred stirred in her heart, until she looked at Father's handsome face on his wedding day.

He had loved her. That mattered. Nothing could be brought back now, but the memories Karalee had could never be snatched from her. Never!

She put the pictures back and covered them up. She had grieved again. And this time the grief settled down and a feeling of desire welled up in her. She couldn't change the past but she could make sure the memories never died. How she would do that was not clear, yet she felt a confidence she hadn't had in months. God was up to something.

She carried down the rocking horse and set it at the bottom of the stairs and added a few other items to talk over with Mother. Would they stay or go?

Twelve

The second week of April was unusually warm for that time of year in Michigan. Karalee reveled in it, choosing to sit on the front veranda in the white chairs which had been brought out last week. One of Laura's brothers had retrieved each one at Mother's request and placed them in the front, all six of them—three on either side of the wide stairs which led up to the beautiful verandah that ran the entire length of the house and around both corners.

Mother sat out in them on nice days and it seemed to improve her health. She had even taken a walk down the street and commented on the buds coming out on the trees, and added that very soon they would be in a more beautiful setting with hanging moss and green, green trees. "Much greener than here," she'd said. "And nothing beats our beautiful Dogwood and Magnolia trees."

Karalee was committed to what lay ahead. She and Jackson waved at each other when he happened by, which was not much these days, and he tipped his hat, but didn't stop anymore. She rarely saw Lily either, but spent more time with Julianne. Mr. Rutledge's house had been the station for his governor-elect followers and it was constantly full of company from all parts of the state. Most of the locals, however, stayed clear, after the incident. Talk had died down, as it usually does, and life had moved on. Visits to Julianne had been Karalee's redemption from all the negativity at home. They had become as close as sisters. Karalee was glad for her friendship and Julianne had actually blossomed right before her eyes. She was now a salaried secretary to Mr. Rutledge. A new maid had been hired to take her place.

Over tea one May morning Julianne had informed her that Mr. Rutledge had asked her to marry him.

"What?" Karalee heard her cup hit the saucer hard. "Are you considering it?" she asked incredulously.

"As I do with all things regarding Mr. Rutledge, I am considering it," she said firmly.

"Please tell me you are not," Karalee pleaded with her friend. "You know his past. You know his weakness for women."

"That I do. But as you can see, he is not a man who can chase a woman these days."

"True," Karalee conceded that fact.

"Julianne, you can have any man you want. And you meet so many. Couldn't you choose any one of them? Perhaps go off with a soldier and live on a farm, have children."

Julianne looked at her and smiled. "And would you do that?"

Karalee had to admit, "Of course, it's none of my business." But thought she would indeed do that and said so.

Julianne smiled and poured Karalee another cup of tea. "What of you? You haven't mentioned Jackson and I haven't seen him around town."

Karalee shrugged and felt guilty. She hadn't talked to her friend about her feelings. "I have been struggling, Julianne. He just seems to have backed off and I'm not sure why. I don't know what I did."

"What if you didn't do anything? What if the problem was his?"

Women's intuition kicked in. "Have you heard something?"

Julianne said, "I was waiting for you to tell me, but I have heard some things."

Karalee put her cup down. "Tell me."

"There's talk he has a boy living with him now."

"A boy?"

"Yes, about eight years old. People are whispering it's his son."

"What?" Karalee stared at her friend. "You are not just hearing gossip?"

"No, I have seen the boy once. When I was at the Milliner's he rode by."

Karalee felt shock, then pain like a knife in her heart. "He couldn't tell me," she whispered. "He didn't trust me."

"Don't blame yourself. I suggest you go visit Lily. I've heard some things people remember about their family. Why don't you pay her a visit?"

Karalee nodded and suddenly needed to go.

"Go, don't listen to any gossip. Find out for yourself, Karalee. I've learned that being truthful from the beginning saves a lot of pain later."

Karalee processed Julianne's words and stood, stopped and turned, "Remember your own words, Julianne, please. Be sure before you give Mr. Rutledge an answer. You will be married to a man who will never walk again...and perhaps never have children."

Julianne nodded solemnly. Momentous times for both of them, Karalee sensed it as she embraced her friend. "God bless you, Julianne."

"And you, Karalee."

She slipped out the door and walked down the street, dazed. One thing she would do before she left was get to the bottom of it. She hated secrets and wondered why Jackson had obviously not trusted her enough to share his own burdens. A visit to Lily was on the way, but she needed a few days to collect her emotions.

Karalee walked in the door and pulled out a recipe from the drawer in the kitchen. Time to bake a couple of lemon cakes. She had to stay busy.

The cakes wrapped and safely stored in the icebox, she finished off the attic. Not one item was left behind. She had carried everything down, except the heavy bedstead, which Laura's brothers were kind enough to move. All of it lay in the parlor. Mother hated the mess but Karalee thought she needed to see it all to decide which things would go or stay. Mother wanted none of it. Not even her wedding picture. Karalee had gone to her room over that one. How could one person be so uncaring?

She'd had to work on her attitude for two days. Then she determined on the twentieth day of April, the most beautiful day thus far, to pay a visit to Lily.

It was time. She took one of the cakes out of the ice box, wrapped it in a clean towel and tucked it into a basket. Karalee decided she was walking today. She'd had Rosebud out for a walk earlier in the morning, but right now she needed to walk, think and pray that whatever happened, she'd be willing to accept.

Thirteen

By the time Karalee arrived at Lily's house she had almost talked herself out of stopping. Lily had not been around either. Her thoughts decidedly split into a hundred different schisms. When she knocked on the door, she could smell coffee.

"Karalee. Come in. I was hoping you'd stop by."

Her first instinct was to ask why she hadn't been in touch, but then she pressed her lips together.

"I've brought Mama's lemon cake."

"Oh how I could use that right now." Lily smiled. "I'll get tea."

In a few minutes they were talking like before. Karalee began to relax and then Lily invited her to sit in the small room near the fire in one of the two rockers. Was this to be the talk she had dreaded?

"Karalee, I know I haven't been around much. I have been rather busy."

"Yes, I understand," she said quietly, then waited.

Lily picked a dead leaf off of a plant sitting on a tall stand and turned to her.

"I think perhaps that you should talk to Jackson."

Karalee hesitated then spoke. "I have, as he was going to town once or twice. It's okay, Lily, if . . . if he doesn't, well, want to see me anymore. I would understand."

"I don't think it's that, in fact I'm sure it's not, Karalee. But I don't feel I can be the one to speak. Shall we talk of other things? I wanted to ask you about who would take care of your lovely flowers on the verandah this summer. Those pots of geraniums always look so beautiful every year."

Karalee felt a shock of disappointment but continued to talk about other things. When it was time to leave, she felt Lily wanted to say more, but didn't.

"Please come again. Spring is here and I know you are leaving soon."

"Yes, we hope no later than June. It will be hot traveling, but Mother can be settled by fall and then I hope to come back."

"So you've no desire to live in a warmer climate?"

"No, nor do I wish to leave my home, if I can manage it alone."

"I'm glad to hear it," Lily said and Karalee knew their conversation was over.

Well, that was not like I thought it would be. She made sure she had walked far enough away from the house to whisper it into the air. *I'm no better off than I was before.* Something wasn't right with Jackson. If he had a child, that's what Lily didn't feel right about telling her. Karalee, when she thought about it, appreciated that.

It was quite a long walk out to Lily and Jackson's and as life would have it, when she came around the last curve in the road, she saw his wagon pulled into her yard beside the house. What was he doing *here*?

She followed voices and could tell they were coming from Rosebud's stall. Her heart beat double time. She sensed today would tell if she and Jackson had a thread left of what she thought she'd seen in him the day he kissed her.

She dropped the basket, which Lily had insisted she fill with flower seeds and a few dried spices she had grown in her garden, on the steps of the verandah. That done, Karalee made her way to the back of the house and could hear Jackson talking quietly about how to muck out a stall.

Karalee thought her heart would burst. His voice was calm and kind. She waited, not wanting to interrupt, and then turned to tiptoe away when she heard her name in that deep voice.

She turned back. "Jackson," she said simply. She could see the leaves above his head swaying in the wind as they stood in the side yard.

"I wanted to stop by and check on Rosebud. No one answered my knock so I came around back."

A boy came out from behind Jackson, and stood very close to him. Karalee almost gasped. He was a miniature version of Jackson.

"James, this is Miss Karalee Williams."

"How do, miss," he said quietly.

"Miss Williams, this is my son, James."

Karalee focused on James as soon as she could pull her eyes away from Jackson's.

"Hello, James. You've met Rosebud I see?"

"I sure have."

"Would you like to ride him ... if it's okay?"

"Can I?" James looked up to Jackson.

"Sure. If Miss Williams says you can, it's okay."

Karalee watched as the two of them drew Rosebud out of the barn, brushed her down and then as Jackson saddled her. When he lifted James and put him in the saddle and handed him the reins, Karalee thought she would break down.

Jackson *was* a father.

She looked on as he circled James around on Rosebud so they could get used to each other. Then he let go of the reins and came to stand by her as they watched James manage the horse.

"Rosebud's behaving properly today," she said.

Jackson looked down at her.

Karalee thought she might have to sit, her knees had weakened. Fears rose up, but her heart longed to tell him how she felt.

Finally after a few rounds, Jackson asked if he might take James to the road for a longer ride.

Karalee smiled. "Of course. I've got to attend to Mother. I have some lemon cake in the house if you'd like."

"When we come back," he said.

Jackson was his old self. She hurried upstairs, pulled off her dusty dress and changed into another one, a simple printed cotton housedress. She didn't want to overdo it. Then a quick visit with Mother and an announcement that Jackson would be coming in for cake. She did not mention James.

"I am not up for guests today," she mumbled. "Shut the door and do not disturb me, Karalee, I have been ill all day."

Mother was disappointed with her. She'd been home alone and not feeling well.

Karalee pulled in a deep breath and shut off the negative connotation her mother was so good at, set a pot of water on the stove, took the cake out of the ice box and put it on one of Mother's fancy plates. She cut it in nice thick servings and plated a few slices of ham they had cooked for breakfast, and then added four biscuits. It would have to do.

Children were always hungry, or so she'd heard.

Time passed long enough for her to hear the grandfather clock strike four.

Not ten minutes later, there were voices out back. Then a knock at the back door. She went and opened it.

"There you are. I thought perhaps you had stolen my horse and ran off," Karalee said brightly.

James looked at his father in fear.

"She was just joshing with you, James." He ruffled his hair.

Karalee saw relief in the young boy's eyes. "I'm sorry, you would never steal a horse would you?"

"No, miss. Never. My ma..."

Jackson interrupted, "James needs to wash up. We put Rosebud back in her stall and gave her a good brush-down," he said quickly.

"James, the wash bowl is right over there. Your father will help you. There's a towel on the hook up high."

She left them to it and felt a surge of sadness when the boy talked about his mother. Karalee wondered what she looked like, but figured she didn't have the right to know anymore right now, so she busied herself setting out the coffee and straining her tea leaves quickly. There was coffee for Jackson, milk for James.

Karalee sipped her tea and watched them eat. Two hungry guys. She smiled, her hands, laying in her lap. "Aren't you going to eat?" Jackson stopped.

"I just had cake with Lily."

Jackson's dark eyes met hers. He wanted to say something, but refrained.

Karalee knew his unasked question. It would have to wait.

After the ham was gone and half the cake, Jackson suggested they help clean up and head back home.

When he sent James to wash his face in the washbowl, then outside to check on Rosebud, he asked Karalee if he might come by tomorrow for a talk, just the two of them.

"Of course," she said and felt his sleeve touch her arm. A tingle went up her back. She put some distance between them, dried the last dish, reached up and placed it on the ledge above.

How quickly a girl could feel heat crawl up and warm her face when a man was around. Not just any man. Mr. Rutledge had given her the opposite feeling when he was nearby.

James came back in and Jackson gave him the once-over...then announced him clean. "What have you to say?"

"Thank you, Miss Williams," James said. "I would like to ride Rosebud again, if you don't mind."

Jackson smiled slightly.

"You may anytime, James," she said and looked into a pair of eyes, much like those of the man standing tall beside him.

The next minute they were taking the back door out. She stood at the front window and watched two figures sitting on the wagon heading home.

Her heart felt alive again.

Fourteen

Everything had changed. Jackson seemed like his old self. She had no idea how all this had come about but Jackson was coming today. He hinted that he would come alone. Karalee fished through her combs and found the perfect set.

She chose a dress, one he had seen her in before, but she cared not a whit. It was a soft green, full dress with three layers of ruffles around the bottom, from her summer stock. The elbow-length sleeves were perfect for spring and the layered collar around her neck had matching ruffles. It was simple and yet quietly elegant. Mother hated it, saying it was too plain.

There was no one there to do her hair, so she wound it tightly into a simple bun and held it in place with the two combs, one on each side. It was enough.

The day was sunny with a bit of wind. The first day she could actually throw open the windows. It was, after all, early May. Tea was ready, and coffee for him. She had risen early, unable to sleep, knowing he was coming. He hadn't said when, but it was better to be ready. She managed to save some cornbread from last night's dinner and soup she could warm up if he were hungry.

Calming herself, she prayed, cleaned up the breakfast dishes and dressed, sat down in the parlor and picked up the book she had been reading. Mother was going to a tea. It was scheduled by the Whitcomb sisters, Suzette and Annette. They were the only two of Mother's friends who came for visits. They had insisted, and Karalee had agreed, Mother owed them a visit now that she was up and herself again.

Thankfully, Mother had left for the day. Laura's father had driven Mother to town and helped her inside, promising to come back later in the day after he had cut and picked up his lumber in Vandalia, just a few miles down the road.

Mother had resisted at first, but when Karalee told her that Jackson was coming, she changed her mind. She had no mind to spend the day with him in the house. "You could do much better, Karalee Elizabeth," she had said for the third time as she made her way out the door.

Providence smiled on her today. Karalee felt a moment of guilt but it was quickly gone as she sat near the window, eyes closed, Mother's white lace curtains from Paris tickling her face as they fluttered in the soft wind.

Those would be among the last things packed. Mother loved her French lace curtains.

An hour passed and no sign. But he would come. Jackson always kept his word. Hopefully, he didn't have trouble at the farm.

Laura came running through the yard from next door and knocked on the screen door. "Isn't it pleasant to have the doors open after such a long winter?" She nearly danced through the door.

"I have news!"

Karalee stood, "What is it? She said immediately.

"I have been accepted. Doc has officially made me his assistant."

"What? That is wonderful, Laura."

"I have been studying for weeks, even writing papers and helping him decipher illnesses of patients. He doesn't tell me but asks me what I think is wrong and helps me know what to look for."

"Your faithful service has been rewarded, Laura. I am sorry we will lose you. You have been a godsend for Mother."

"I know you will be leaving, Miss Karalee, but I will miss you and your mother."

"You have served us well. Doc is sending for papers where he studied in Kentucky and I'm learning so much. I cannot get enough of it! But I must not bore you. I understand not everyone cares whether one's appendix is on the left side or the right side." She laughed.

"Indeed they don't. But you do. And that's all that matters. This is what God made you for, Laura."

"I feel the same," she said. "But I must go. Father is coming back late this evening and I must have my studying done. We are fixing up my old room. Mother is expecting another baby."

"How wonderful." Karalee smiled at the sweet-faced young woman. "Go...go study. You must not waste a minute," she said and patted her back.

"I must. But I wanted to tell you first because...you believed in me."

"From the very beginning, Laura."

Karalee received a quick hug and saw the tail of Laura's homemade dress fly out the door. She sat down and filled her lungs with fresh air.

When another hour passed Karalee got up and stretched, went outdoors to wipe off the seats of the rockers in front. The dust and wind had blown new buds up on the verandah and dotted the chairs. If Jackson wished to sit out here, they must be clean.

She had just finished when she heard the wagon, stood with cloth in hand and watched as it came around the bend into view. She would never tire of that scene.

A quick hand wash at the sink and some rose water behind her ears, she waited for the knock. When it did come, she felt her heart jump. Funny how life could look so hopeful some days, like today, and so hopeless on others.

She viewed him through the screen and invited him to come in or if he preferred, they would sit on the rockers. He chose the verandah.

"You've dressed up nicely today," she said by way of compliment. "He shrugged, took his hat off and set it on the rocker next to him, then looked over at her.

"I like that dress," he said simply.

"Thank you." He had noticed.

Suddenly, he lifted his rocker and turned it slightly so he was facing her instead of sitting next to her. "I'm here to set myself straight with you."

Karalee nodded and hoped he wasn't here to say goodbye, he had a son to raise or he wanted to be back with the boy's mother. She had not thought of that until now. Perhaps they had . . .oh, she must not think of it and pressed her hands together in her lap, muscles tight.

"Of course." She turned herself slightly toward him and pushed her shoulders against the flat back of the chair.

He sat for a moment and then said, "I am not good at talking about such things, but Lily told me I had to come clean."

He paused.

"I don't exactly know where to start, I guess from the beginning. Sometime back I was a pretty difficult young kid who didn't act as I should have. My father and I, well, we didn't get along, if you know what I mean."

"How so?" Karalee asked, noting Jackson kept changing the position of his booted feet, like he wanted to run. He looked so nice in church-going clothes that she almost asked where he was headed.

"What was he like—your father?"

"He could be a nice guy to folks he dealt with in public, but he was not the same at home. He, um…treated my mama badly. And Lily would tell you he treated me bad, too, when I tried to stick up for Mama. Things got rough enough that I left when I was sixteen. Never told him where I was going, just left. I went to Ohio to my Uncle Lyon, my mama's oldest brother. He took me in and I worked for him. He treated me right. When I heard several years later that my father died, I didn't come home for the burial."

He paused.

"I wouldn't have, either." Karalee couldn't help herself. "Was your mama okay after you left? And Lily?"

"Yes, Lily said he still said mean things and pushed her around when he got really mad. But Lily was his favorite. She hated that, though. And we both felt bad for Mama. Then when I left . . ."

Karalee could see he was looking for the right words.

"When I left, Lily said he wasn't as angry anymore."

"Why? Because you were a good son?" Karalee shot back.

Jackson laughed a little. "Maybe. I'll never know. All I *do* know is he hated me for some reason."

Her heart breaking, she felt a sheen cover her eyes and stared at the trees out front for a bit before she could speak.

"I didn't say all that to make you feel sorry for me," he said quietly after a time.

"I know. I'm feeling sorry for myself, because I know what it feels like to have a parent be your worst critic," she said, weak-voiced, surprised at her willingness to admit such a thing to herself, let alone Jackson.

"You got that right." He gave her a half smile. "Your mother's a good woman, but she's got a lot of work to do to think of somebody else besides herself."

Karalee could have cried right there. Almost did. She nodded, unable to speak.

"Life throws us mud balls sometimes. We get hit, faces dirtied, hearts-hurting and just plain mad, but like Lily said, what goes around comes around."

"Yes," she admitted and felt a keen kinship. She had never really talked about how Mother hurt her. Father knew, John knew, but no one outside the family. "What happened after your father died?"

"Mama died not long after. Lily and I could never figure out why she was sad he was gone. He was most unkind to her. But she loved him, I guess. That's when I came home."

"I'm so sorry, Jackson."

"Don't be sorry. It was the way it was. I learned a lot while I was gone. Learned to drink, learned to be angry at anyone who tried to force me into anything I didn't want to do, and became downright ugly you might say." He stopped to think a minute and continued. "Next thing you know I met up with Sadie when I had come back. She and I...well, I guess she liked me since the fourth level, but when I took off to Ohio, I didn't even write or anything. When I came back, Lily told me she had waited for me. She and Lily were best friends.

"But I wasn't the same young kid as when I left. She tried to tame me down, but I preferred to drink, and I liked being angry. I had never been able to express myself to my father. He'd cuff me if I tried. So I picked fights anywhere I went.

"Sadie tried. She really did. And when I came drunk one time to pick her up, her father told me he couldn't let me come back.

"I think deep down I was hoping he'd tell me that. Because I knew I wasn't good enough for his daughter.

"At least I didn't destroy her life...or thought I didn't until I found out about James."

At this point Jackson looked down at the gray wood planks and did not make eye contact with her, but kept talking, like something inside him just wouldn't stop.

"I pushed her away," he said quietly. "I wanted her to go so I wouldn't ruin her life. But I swear." He looked up. "I swear I knew nothing about a baby coming."

"Fact is, I was surprised when she up and married Ely Emory, who'd always had his eye on her all through the high levels. But she'd chosen me and I let her down. "Now I know why she had to marry him."

The winds blew Jackson's hair across his face, but Karalee saw he didn't seem to notice and kept on talking.

"After that I just didn't care about anything. Lily told me that Father had taken my name off the deed...mine and Mama's. After she died, I went from town to town for a time. Then Lily wrote me a letter. I always let her know where I was. She told me to come home. She had signed the deed over to me and I had to sign the papers. I refused to come at first until I realized how much I hurt her. She needed help. I came back, but I wasn't easy to be around. Finally, one day she told me she was moving out of Mama and Father's big house and letting me have it all to myself. She packed her things and moved into the cottage house next door."

He smiled slightly. "See what a fool I was, hurting Lily like that. Well, she was having none of it! She was the first one who stood up to me. And I listened to her. So we worked the farm; I handled most of it with hired help, then Tom and Ruth Thompson coming alongside me. As you know, they are Quakers who believe in everybody."

Karalee laughed.

"You sick of this story yet?" Jackson looked her in the eye.

"No. Go on."

"Well, the Thompsons took me aside one day and said if I'd give up drinking they had a favor to ask, if I didn't mind.

"I quit drinking, partly because Lily told me I had to, and partly because I was just plain sick of being mad. Mama was gone, Father was gone. He couldn't hurt me or Mama anymore. But the memories kept eating at me. When I'd been sober six months, Tom and Ruth came over and told me they were helping slaves find freedom... did I want to help? They worried that someone would find them out, so wanted to know if they could use my barn. It was nearer the woods, where theirs was small and stuck right out in the middle of an open field.

"I said I would, not knowing a thing about it. When you found me out that day, I'd been at it for almost two years."

"Oh my," Karalee said softly, opened her mouth and nothing came out except, "Go on."

"Well, I was all set to get you out of the picture. I worried you could get hurt with all the raiders in the area, or worse we'd all be found out. I couldn't let that happen, so I made sure I found fault and got you out of there. Just in time, too. I ended up getting shot and it could have easily been you."

Karalee waited, wanting to know if he cared for her, or if he just needed a friend to help with the work.

"Fact is, I had feelings for you and then when I asked you twice to marry me, you refused.

"You had made up your mind, so I made up mine. I wasn't going to ask again. I decided I'd probably do with you like I had done with Sadie. I'd shut you out because I wasn't sure I'd make you, or anyone else for that matter, a good husband."

"And that was the reason?" Karalee watched his eyes for the truth.

"Yep. That's the story."

She pulled in a huge, fresh lungful of air. For two reasons, because she realized she hadn't taken a full deep breath since he started talking, and because she felt a huge sense of relief. Except for one thing. She had to know.

"How did you find out about James?"

"Ely Emory came to my door a couple months ago and told me Sadie had died."

She clasped her fingers together and looked down at her lap. "I'm sorry, Jackson...for her and for her son."

"Yeah, well, I wasn't too happy about James at first. She never told me. But I wasn't exactly husband material then. I had left right after her father said I couldn't see her again. She never told Ely anything. He thought *he* was the father. Before she died she confessed to him and asked Ely to bring my son to me. At least he would know the truth. Ely's a good man. He didn't have to tell a soul once Sadie was gone. But he kept his word to her, said the boy had a right to know, and if he wanted to come back, Ely would raise him as his own."

71

Not a word came out of her mouth. Her eyes spoke for her. The story was so sad she knew rivulets of tears ran down her face. How miserable and hard the world could be sometimes.

Jackson took a deep breath, ran his fingers through his hair and sat back, sticking his legs out and crossing them at the ankles, his boots nearly touching hers.

She didn't know whether to laugh or cry. Laugh at the fact that God sure had a way of making things right, or cry at the way it had come about.

Jackson sat gazing over her shoulder for a long time. He looked relieved. She felt angst and relief all at once.

Then she heard a wagon pull up. Mama was home.

Karalee ran inside and splashed water in her face. What awful timing.

Laura's father was helping her down from the wagon. Karalee watched from inside the screen door as Jackson got up and brought Mama the rest of the way. Karalee slipped into the kitchen before she could be seen with a red face. Mother would never quit asking questions if she saw she'd been crying.

"Why don't you lie down and rest?" Jackson took her to her room and asked if she needed anything. Karalee guessed she didn't because he came back to find her in the kitchen, and as soon as he walked in she turned her back, put her face in her hands, and sobbed.

A minute later, she felt his strong hands on her arms and as he gently turned her around, she threw hers around his middle and hid her face in his shoulder.

Fifteen

Three full days passed. Karalee walked around in a daze, working, walking to town for stationery. Mama was writing letters to her parents' address in Charleston, should they be there, and another to the Ohio address letting them know she was coming two months hence. Karalee walked through daily duties like always but hardly remembered them when she finished.

"What is wrong with you? I told you to bring me two boxes of writing papers. Now you'll have to make another trip."

"You did?"

"Yes, I wrote it down. Are you ill?"

"No Mother, I'm not ill," she said without anger. "I'll go again. I need fresh air."

Jackson had left that day. Left her... standing in the kitchen feeling bereft without his arms around her, and wondering how she would live if they were never together again. Karalee needed Jackson Clay Woodridge...James too, and now she was on the way to Charleston. How had that happened? She was ready to go, but now she didn't want to leave. What would become of her and Jackson? She had to see Julianne.

She was glad Mother needed more paper, plus she asked her to stop and purchase the blue feathered hat in the Millinery window, *before Mrs. Smythe bought it out from under her nose.* Karalee was glad to oblige. "I'll hurry on over, Mother."

When she walked into the store, Mrs. Smythe had just bought it. Well, that was that. Mother would be livid. Mrs. Smythe was the one woman in town Mother envied. Karalee was glad for the diversion, but knew she'd never hear the end of this anytime soon. She had failed again. But now it seemed rather silly and funny all at once. She bought the stationery and hurried over to Julianne's.

73

Mr. Rutledge was in meetings again, but Julianne was free for an hour, she said. She had letters to write and mail later that afternoon. Important ones.

"This running for Governor thing has many loopholes," Julianne declared and sat down in a huff, her hands flying through the air and landing in her lap.

Karalee gave her friend a minute to recover.

"You look positively glowing," Julianne said, still breathless. "Why are you here?" She squinted her eyes, reached for her handkerchief just inside the sleeve at her wrist, and dabbed her cheeks and forehead. "It is warm already and spring has just begun."

"Yes it has."

"Well?" Julianne prompted her.

"Jackson came and we had a long talk."

Julianne scooted closer to the edge of her seat. "And?"

"I think he still cares for me."

"You think? Didn't he declare it?"

"In so many words. I'm leaving in a month."

"Karalee Williams. He should declare himself before you leave or he might lose you."

"Well, it's not quite like that. You see three days ago he came and told me all. All about his life, what it was like, why he was the way he was, all of it." Karalee stood and walked to the window.

"My gracious, men are slow to understand," Julianne sputtered as she stood.

"Hmmm....sounds like you have a dilemma yourself," Karalee baited her friend.

"Indeed I do. But it will wait." She swung her hand in an arc then sat down again." Forgive me, I am overwhelmed today. You must take me as I am. So if Jackson does ask for your hand, will you accept?"

"I will," Karalee said quietly.

"Then see, it is done, except to wait for the proposal."

"I hope that's what will happen. The thing is, Julianne, he does have a child."

"It's as I heard then. It wasn't just silly gossip?"
"No, but he told me all. And I understand him."

"Then if you are fine, don't worry a single minute what others think. It doesn't really matter."

"You are right." Karalee turned her head.

"What is that look?"

"That look, my dear friend, is admiration. You are wonderful. You speak truth and you care not a whit what others think. I should like to be more like you, Julianne."

"Oh puff, you already are you ninny, you just don't see it. Now be off with you. Get home. Jackson might make his proposal. And I must get back to work. We will chat. Because I also have news."

"Do tell me now!" Karalee said as she stood.

"I cannot. I don't have the answer yet. But you will be first to know. Now go. I cannot afford to be sacked."

Karalee found she was standing alone and made her way out. She walked slowly, enjoying the spring branches of the newly budded trees, the smell of freshness in the air after the long winter. She dreaded telling Mother about the hat.

When she had just set foot on the verandah, she gasped. Jackson and James were sitting there in the chairs. "I didn't know you were coming."

"We didn't either," Jackson said, took off his hat, looked at James who took his off, and then they both stood.

"I am just back from downtown. Would you like a lemonade?"

James looked to his father. At his nod they came through the door and straight into the kitchen.

"Is that you, Karalee? Did you get the hat?"

"I'll be there in a few minutes Mother." Then whispered, "I didn't get it!"

Jackson actually laughed. "Well then, as soon as we're done here we're going to ask if we might take Rosebud on a *long* walk today."

"Please do," Karalee said and shushed them when they both laughed. As soon as they had consumed their lemonade, she sent them out the back and quietly shut the door.

Once she saw the dust rising as Jackson on Stockton, and James on Rosebud were heading out toward his place, she splashed some water on her face, gathered her packages and went in to give Mother first her stationery, and then the news.

True to form, Mother had a conniption fit. She got up out of her bed and would not be comforted. "How dare she come in and get it. She knew I wanted that hat."

"How would she know, Mother?" Karalee said softly.

"She always knows, that woman. Why, if she thinks her blood is bluer than mine, I've got news for her. I'm bluer-blooded than she'll ever be."

The deed done, Karalee knew there would be no peace for the rest of the day and went up, changed into her working-in-the-garden-dress and began pulling out old leaves and branches out front. Every year Father did it and she would do it now. It was not only necessary, it soothed her just knowing it would be the way he would have liked. There would be no time to plant flowers and no one would be here to water them. Oh Lord, how was she ever going to leave?

Sixteen

Another week passed so quickly it made Karalee sick to her stomach. She and Jackson had had little time to sit down and talk after that wonderful day. He had acres of ground to break, a child to look after, plus corn and wheat to plant.

Mother had finally heard from her parents. They were allowed back home immediately after Lee surrendered to Grant in April. But said the getting there was the worst of it.

And their house, by God's grace was still standing. It had been used as a Union headquarters.

Mother had been livid about that. Yankees in her house! Her beloved Drayton Manor! How dare they? Karalee had not heard the end of it, but worse was the fact that Mrs. Smythe had spread all over town she had bought that blue feathered hat right out from underneath that snobbish, near murderess Mrs. Williams.

It was all Karalee could think about…glad they were leaving. The fire that hat started was not likely to be put out anytime soon.

For all of Mother's talk of blueblood connections, Karalee felt sorry for her. She saw her mother in a new light. Mother had not enjoyed a single day of life. And she had ruined the lives of most everyone she was supposed to love. Heaven forbid that Grandaddy and Granmama crossed her in their old age. The only thing Mother would be satisfied with was if she were in her childhood home. Drayton Manor would forever be the place she wanted to be. Karalee felt she could at least do that for her.

Resigned to it, she prepared her heart and mind to leave her only home, but more than that, Jackson and James. They had come by almost every day to ride Rosebud. She had first asked Jackson privately, and with his permission asked James if he would keep

Rosebud for her while she was gone. Jackson had given her that warm look, the one she remembered in earlier days.

By the time Rosebud was back in her stall later in the afternoon, Mother had taken a walk and calmed herself once she realized she wouldn't have to lay eyes on that *pompous* Mrs. Smythe's face ever again. She wouldn't be around to see that hat. "That should fix her. Take the wind right out of her sails," Mother told her daughter upon returning home and, tired from her walk, shut the door to nap.

Her mother was getting weaker, it seemed, not stronger. She still depended on the medicine Doc gave her. He lessened the dose, but Mother knew right away and insisted he give her what she needed. Finally Doc told Karalee that he was giving her a little powder, but mixing in small increases of corn powder just to make it look right, hoping he could wean her off.

Karalee had shaken her head and apologized with her eyes the best she could. She and Doc did what they had to do to keep the peace.

Before Karalee was ready, it was a week until they would be leaving. The house had been cleared of every single item Mother wanted back home. Many trips to the train station had sent the trunks on their way. Karalee only hoped, with the war-torn south, that Mother's things made it there in one piece. Especially her dishes.

The closets were cleaned and finally Karalee had packed most of her belongings, which amounted to several dresses, night clothes and underthings, two pairs of shoes, and a coat in the event of rain, plus two of her favorite hats. She did not intend to stay, in fact had left her journal beneath the floorboard. She dared not take it along. Mother would find it and have no trouble reading every word. Instead she found a small book at the stationery store and purchased it. She would still have to make sure Mama didn't find it. She would blow up like a steam engine if she read a single page.

Still, Karalee saw her Mother was sad. She could see it in her eyes at breakfast and throughout the day. She had taken more walks, too, like she might even miss Cassopolis, Michigan after all.

"You and John were born here," she said one afternoon while working on her embroidery, preferring to be up instead of resting her bad leg. Doc had said she must get exercise or an ugly scar would form near the entry of the wound. Mother had taken it to heart.

"Are you sure you want to go?" Karalee asked quietly as mother worked while she read.

What she received was a hard stare over the top of her mother's spectacles. Karalee blinked and continued reading.

Two days later, several folks came to say goodbye to Mother and wish her well. Laura's entire family fit themselves in the parlor, and then the pastor and his wife, plus several members from the church stopped by. Even though Mother rarely attended the church they treated her kindly and said they'd pray for a safe trip. She had harrumphed at that, saying when the good Lord was ready to take her, he wouldn't be listening to any of those prayers they were all praying. Karalee thanked them anyway.

Jackson came two days before their leaving. Alone. He asked Karalee to step outside. Mother overhead and said from the other room, "What do you two have to talk about anyway? We'll be gone soon."

Karalee motioned for Jackson not to answer and followed him out the door. He looked tired and his face was darker already from the spring sun.

"I'm here because I can't let you and your mother make the trip alone. I've arranged for James to stay with Lily. I'm going with you."

"Jackson, you can't leave your farm. It's time to plant and your fields aren't even cleared."

"Tom and I cleared them yesterday."

"Who will plant all those acres?"

"I've got a few friends. I'll make sure you both get there and then we will come back together."

"I don't know how long I'll need to stay. Word is there's so much damage to Charleston, Mother may not be able to stay."

"Be that as it may, you two are not going alone. You're Yankees, well, at least you are. Your Mother will burn the ears of any Confederate who accuses her of being a Yankee." He laughed. "But you, I don't want you finding yourself in somebody's debt and not knowing who you can trust."

"Jackson, I am not afraid. I have prayed myself silly and somehow I know that whatever happens, I'll be all right. Everyone has lost loved ones. Be they Confederate or Yankee, it doesn't matter. Somehow I know God will watch over us."

79

He looked away and back again.

"Don't you have any guests coming?" She used their secret language like before.

"Haven't for a while. Once the Yankees broke through down there, the slaves were joining up with them by the thousands. They had a place to run to. I think we're done up here. Especially since Lee surrendered. Thank God the war is over, Karalee."

"All the more reason for you to stay here and work your farm. I'll be back as soon as I can. I'm sure the rebuilding in the South has begun and will be further along by the time we get there. I'm hoping only a few weeks."

Jackson nodded and listened. He felt stubborn. Didn't like being told no, but what she said made sense. By the time harvest time came she would be back. And he wouldn't have to leave James so soon. It had been a hard adjustment at first. He had talked about his mother and missed her terribly. Ely had come down once, but it confused James. He felt sad that Ely didn't have someone at his house anymore. That had been difficult. His young son, worried about Ely, the only father he knew.

Sadie, and Ely for that matter, had done a good job raising James. Jackson had finally told Ely he owed him a huge debt and would never be able to repay it. The best he could do was make sure James visited the man he had thought was his father since he was born.

It was a strange thing, though—Jackson pondered many a day sitting on his tractor—that James would so easily adapt to his new home and to him. He couldn't help but wonder if God had been in it all the time, yet at the same time, could not understand why God had allowed his father to hate him so much. How could a man hate his own son?

Seventeen

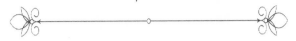

Somehow, Karalee managed to talk Jackson into staying behind. She and Mother would make it all right. It would be tough, but at least they only had two trunks apiece since everything else had gone ahead. He insisted he would be the one to drive them to the train depot in Niles. The Michigan Central line would take them to Chicago, and then South to Atlanta.

Jackson got help carrying in the trunks, his shoulder still not fully healed. When he returned, he stood by while Karalee paid for their tickets. The man behind the window stamped each one three times and they were officially on their way. It was the sixth of June.

Mother made a trip to the ladies room. Karalee stood by and held her satchel.

"It's a beautiful day," she felt her voice wobble and looked out to the stand of trees on the other side of the track. When Mother returned, Jackson took Karalee's arm and said firmly, "We'll be right back." Mother gave him her famous disapproving look.

Once outside, Jackson held onto her elbow and stepped under the nearest tree. Then before she knew what happened, he had doffed his hat and with his eyes looking into hers, slowly leaned down and kissed her. She felt his hair tickle her forehead. Next thing she knew he hatted his head and with a wink, took her arm and brought her back inside. Just as if nothing had happened.

Her face burned as they passed two couples who had knowing smiles on their faces. She could not utter a word.

When they joined Mother, he leaned down and whispered he liked her dress. "That blue and black plaid print suits you," he said quietly, smiling at her discomfort. Karalee tried to ignore him. Her face was still burning scarlet from that kiss.

Suddenly, she lost a chunk of courage; should she leave him? But how could she stay? Mama couldn't travel alone. Perhaps she should have let Jackson come, but that would be selfish. She admonished her weakness and straightened her back. If it was meant to be, it would be.

Jackson took Mother to her seat first and came back for her. He settled their satchels on the shelf above. He was in the way of oncoming passengers, so tipped his hat to Mother and wished her well, then to Karalee with a smile meant only for her, and he was gone. Karalee felt a new bereavement overtake her.

Once the train started moving slowly away from the station, blowing smoke as it went and chugging down the track, she finally felt her heart settle. She had a mission. And that was one thing she loved: a purpose, something that mattered. Mother was going home.

While Mother slept she turned her thoughts to the work ahead. Grandaddy and Granmama had written they had hired locals to clean out the house and rid it of anything having to do with those Yankees, and they were starting to make progress. They had ordered Mother's childhood room to be cleaned first so she had a place to sleep. Karalee could see why Mother was so spoiled.

Their family had strong blood ties from their ancestors—Generals, Doctors and Statesmen—Grandaddy said, and they *would* recover. Fact was, Mama's family had lots of money and that's what helped them get back on their feet. Karalee had seen photos of the war-ravaged city in newspapers and wasn't as convinced all was the pretty picture they had painted, so prepared herself for the worst.

The train ride had been wonderful, but when they arrived in Atlanta the tracks were all but gone. From there they had to take a stagecoach and there was hardly any room because of the influx of people coming back home.

Eight days and two changes in conveyances; rain, dust and full-to-overflowing hotels along the way, and they were almost there. "A hundred miles, Mama," Karalee said tiredly. "You're almost home."

Mother had only groaned. If she wasn't ranting about something, it was a sure sign she was worn out. Doc had secretly given Karalee more powders to make sure Mother would make it. But Karalee kept that fact to herself. Mother got her daily dose and managed the train well, until the stagecoach jiggling her across terrible roads for miles on end finally got to her. Karalee had given her extra doses. She had become quiet and slept as much as she could with all the bouncing.

82

Finally, at three o'clock in the morning, the last coach ride brought them to Mother's house the city. The street lights were few and far between. The town was a mess of brick and mortar and tents, yet Karalee thought she'd never seen such a beautiful sight. Her childhood home almost every summer for years: Drayton Manor. The name sign hung over the door, but it was freshly painted. The old one had been worn after years near the ocean. This plaque was fairly new.

Mother didn't even notice. She required assistance managing the coach stairs and nearly fell in the doing of it. Grandaddy scolded the manservant who was doing his best, having just been called from his bed in the middle of the night.

Karalee quietly thanked him.

There was hardly time for greetings and hugs. The smell of burning wood and rotten fish hung heavy in the warm, damp air. Karalee could hardly breathe. Mother was so spent she had wanted to sleep on the divan downstairs, but Granmama would have none of it. She said with a firm voice, "Kathryn, you can walk a few more steps."

Karalee tucked Mother's arm in her elbow as they went step by step up and around the long, wide curvature of the grand staircase. It was no small feat for Mother to drag herself up dozens of steps. What saddened Karalee most was to hear the same, disrespectful expectation in Granmama's voice as Karalee had heard in her mother. She hadn't remembered that when she was young.

Grandaddy waited until they were up and then turned off the lights. Karalee let Mother lead her to her old room. She had forgotten which of the several doors in the curved upper level was the right one.

Mother gasped as she opened the door, slowly. Her eyes swept the room in one slow turn of her head. Karalee let her have her moment, and then noticed tears falling from Mother's eyes. Karalee had rarely seen that.

"Let's get you in your gown, Mother."

"No. Relieve me of my coat, these stockings and awful shoes. My feet hurt. I will sleep in my underthings. It's much too hot."

Karalee did as her Mother bid, closed the door behind her and found the manservant waiting in his white coat and black pants, hands down at his sides. He bowed slightly, and said, "Follow me, Miss Karalee."

"How did you know my name?"

"Oh, I done heard all 'bout ya," he said kindly. "Ya must be awful tired."

"I am. What is your name?"

He looked at her for a moment before he answered. "I'd be Hudson Jones."

"Well, Hudson, thank you for getting out of your bed at this dreadful hour. I'm sure you'll be rising when the sun comes up...just as we are going to sleep."

"Dat be the truth, miss," he said with a quiet chuckle, stopped and stood by a door, opening it for her. "Ya need sometin', Miss Glory be up in just a minute. I be gettin' dat satchel for you."

He set it inside her door and was gone.

Eyes burning from dust all day long, she looked around, took off her short traveling cape and laid it over a chair back, making sure not to shake it out. The dust would fill up the room.

A quiet knock produced a very young girl. "You must be Glory?"

"Yes, miss. Would ya like me to run the bath, ma'am?"

"Oh no, but thank you."

Glory had already set her satchel on the trunk at the end of the four-poster bed and opened it, then stood aside.

Karalee was not used to servants.

"I will be fine, please go back to your bed."

"Yes, miss," Glory said and didn't move.

"I'm sorry I didn't mean to tell you what to do."

A slight smile lit up Glory's face. "It be my job to see to ya."

"Thank you, but all I want is to get into my night clothes and climb into bed."

"I'll just turn yo bed down den and leave ya be."

Karalee took a deep breath. "That would do just fine."

Glory did a few extra things before she left: closed the curtains against the morning sun, filled the water pitcher on the table next to the bed, set a glass nearby and with a last look, slipped out the door.

She was so quiet Karalee hardly knew she was there. Alone, at last, she undressed and put on her cotton shift, glad she had not brought anything heavier. The summer nights were already thick with heat in Charleston.

Eighteen

Morning came, but one would not have known it. The heavy curtains had so darkened the room, a person couldn't tell if it were day or night. With a stretch, Karalee wakened slowly, threw off the top counterpane and stayed abed. Her legs, arms and back ached from the long journey. Quickly, she located the in-room commode and did her business, rinsed her hands off in the bowl and slid back a curtain. A bright light jabbed her eyes, burning them. She shut the curtains but left a tiny sliver so she could see in the room.

It was so elegant. She couldn't remember being in this part of the house. She and John had mostly played outside, ridden horses and spent time in the ocean. How lucky they had been. The grandness of the house had missed her attention as a child. The dollhouse on the summer porch out back, the gardens with pretty flowers, and most especially the sailboats lined up by the hundreds rocking on the water—these stayed in her memory. John had loved sailing. He, Father and Grandaddy would spend the whole day out, while the ladies attended tea functions, shopped in the tiny specialty stores and sat on summer chairs in the English garden. The ones with the rock paths. She had skipped through them many times, the fragrances strong in the summer heat.

So many memories. A slight knock at the door and Glory slipped through the crack to greet her. "I run yo bath."

"You did? When?"

"While ya be sleepin'," she said looking a bit worried.

"Thank you! I need a bath terribly."

Glory's face relaxed and she led her to the bathroom wherein were beautiful tiled walls and floors, a huge bathtub with pipes coming out of the wall, and the commode.

"De water still be warm, miss. But if ya like it hot I be bringin' up more water.

"No need, I'm sure it's fine." Karalee waited for her to leave.

"I be here to help with yo bath, wash yo hair, what ya like."

Karalee's eyes widened. "I'll be fine, but thank you." She remembered the maid helping her with her bath as a child, but was surprised she would be offered the task of helping her now.

"Would you mind bringing tea? And toast and eggs, if the kitchen is open."

"Miss, it be way past noon. It be open since early dis mornin'."

"Noon?" Karalee knew her mouth was open. "Is Mother, Mrs. Williams up?"

"No miss, she says she wants to sleep til tomorrow, but soon as ya come out, she wants to see ya."

"Thank you, Glory. Please tell her I'll be there within the hour."

"Yes, miss."

And Glory was gone.

Not wishing to rush, Karalee dropped her clothes on the bathroom floor. She didn't want dust on the beautiful wood floors in the bedroom. The water was warm and welcoming. The soap smelled of roses. She relished the bath and dunked her full head of hair beneath the water and washed it, then laid her head back on a rolled cloth and shut her eyes. She was so far away.

Sometime later, she opened her eyes and raised her head. She must make herself move. She felt like a fish in water; she didn't want to get out, but with no way to tell the time, she stood, toweled off and patted her hair dry.

Glory announced her presence not long after and wondered if Karalee would like help combing out her hair.

"You know, Glory, I think I might. Just a moment, I'll be out." She wrapped herself in the huge towel and slipped into a fresh gown and sat for Glory to brush out her hair.

"That feels so good. I've not had my hair brushed in forever," she said with a sigh.

"Yo hair's big. I be thinkin' of rollin' it in rags tonight for 'dem long curls like someone done wrapped each one around a stick," she chuckled.

Karalee smiled, wishing Glory could do that right now. She wouldn't have minded a bit. "Men down here like de women with long hair," Glory said with a serious tone.

86

"Do they now? If you'd like to come back tonight, perhaps you could roll my hair."

"Yes, miss," she said.

Karalee loved her straight, firm answers.

"Right now, yo mama is waitin' for ya below stairs."

Karalee knew what that meant. "You go ahead, and I'll be done in a little while. Would you please tell her?"

"I be doin' dat, miss." And Glory was gone again.

It was a good thing Karalee was used to dressing herself because Glory would be doing it all if she'd let her.

When she had finished, she dipped to check her face in the mirror and saw how Glory had done her hair. She had combed it strand by strand and pressed a dry cloth to it over and over until it was not wet, just damp. She had arranged it nicely.

When Karalee stepped out of her room, she took the stairs slowly, her legs still aching and stiff. She could hear murmurings and walked to the dining room, noting the familiar wallpaper down the hall. Mother, Grandaddy and Granmama were all sitting at the long cherry table with the beautiful embroider-backed chairs, talking. The three of them looked small around the huge table. More memories flooded back.

"I've been waiting for you," Mother said, and motioned for her to sit to her right. Instantly, another servant was at her side pouring tea into her cup. The sugar and tongs were there, as was a tiny pitcher of cream.

"Toast and eggs, miss?"

"Yes, please."

When brunch was finished the four of them went out to the planetarium. It had looked so large as a child, but in relation to the other parts of the house, looked quite small. Two men were busy working on it. She could see it had fallen into ruin.

Her grandparents took her and Mother for a tour, telling what all was being done to bring their beloved Drayton Manor back to its original elegance. There was much talk of Yankees during that time, her grandparents forgetting she carried both Yankee and Confederate blood.

Karalee ignored it. It wasn't her house that had been ravaged. She understood.

They then headed out of the planetarium since it was still an eyesore and out into the English gardens. Karalee almost gasped. The only thing there was the tiny rock strewn pathways. A few straggly plants survived, but it was nothing like she remembered. The talk, of course, went the same direction, how they were going to restore it. It was sad.

There was a half circle bench beneath a low hanging tree. The green of the leaves was vivid. Karalee took a seat there while the others went out into the back part of the yard and then through a gate. It was a path that led to the water in an offhand sort of way. One had to work their way around the back of the house and then cross the street. Houses were not generally placed on the waterside, in the event hurricanes blew in.

The grounds, even though not as they had been, were repairable. She enjoyed sitting in the shade while the low branches tumbled in the breeze, and wondered how Jackson and James were doing. They were so far away.

Nineteen

The days passed slowly at first and then began to fly by. Everyone needed some type of help. Workmen had flooded into town. There was so much damage to the buildings that some were afraid to enter their churches, banks or businesses, worried they would fall in on them. More buildings were crumbled than standing.

Trash and debris were hauled away. It seemed a never-ending scene as wagons of all shapes and sizes rattled past on the cobblestone streets carrying bricks and posts, even furniture that had been burned.

Karalee spent many a morning on the front verandah. People usually stopped to gaze at the few houses that had survived, mostly because they were the biggest and held the most officers. Her grandparents were some of the lucky ones, but after a time, Karalee wondered if they realized it. They complained about every little thing.

No wonder Mother was so critical.

In time, two or three ladies would stop by at first for a chat as they happened by, and then stay for tea on the white-washed verandah. Mother seemed to enjoy that and even recognized two of her former classmates who had never left Charleston. That kept her busy, and Karalee enjoyed watching her get better every day. If that kept up, she could head back home in a few weeks.

Meanwhile, she wrote two letters to Jackson and had not heard back from him, although it had only been two weeks. Then again, mail service was strictly big city to big city. Folks living in outlying areas had to drive for miles to pick up their mail. But Charleston was especially damaged. There was too much reconstruction going on.

Yet she saw the hearts of the people. Charleston would be better and finer than it had ever been. She heard that talk many a day.

Finally, two months into her stay, a letter arrived. A wonderful man who'd sadly lost his wife and daughter in the war, needed work, so took his wagon overland to Atlanta and brought back mail and supplies two times a month. It was three hundred miles each way. By the time he arrived there he had to turn around and come right back.

Grateful, Karalee opened the thin envelope with her nail. She unfolded the letter across her knees and read. All was well. Jackson and James had managed to get the corn planted with the help of Thomas and a couple of other neighbors. It was already almost waist high. Rosebud was doing fine. So well, in fact, Jackson mentioned he was worried James would be hard-put to give her back.

She smiled and continued reading. Her house was fine. Laura had planted a few flowers along the front verandah but had to study. She had asked him to *let Karalee know she'd passed her second exam. Julianne says she is going to write.* He saw her at the General Store the day before. That was about it.

The letter, resting on her lap, Karalee looked out over the horizon as the sun was coming down over the water. It was so beautiful here. The sun had warmed the front of the house, and now the purple, orange and pink setting with white sailboats swaying gently on the waves made her wonder if Jackson would love to see this place. And James...

Scenes of home played out in her mind as she rocked and pulled at the collar of her dress. She should go inside or better yet, out to the back side of the house to get some shade!

After a few more weeks, and before autumn settled in Michigan, Karalee hoped to be home. She found her favorite spot under the shade tree on the bench and cracked open a book. A good read, *Count of Monte Cristo*. She'd read it before and because it was Father's favorite, she borrowed it from the library and began to read, wishing she could write as well as its French author, Alexandre Dumas. The mystery, hardships and character-driven desire to get revenge worked its magic as she read.

Then the words on the pages became more difficult to read and Karalee realized it was dusk. She closed the book and wondered that Glory had not come for her. Dinner must be late this evening.

Indeed it was. Someone had stolen the wood from the side yard.

The authorities had been called. The perpetrator, a young boy, was at this moment being interrogated.

Karalee walked to the front of the house where an officer had the boy by the collar of his shirt, what was left of it.

He was trying to explain he and his little sister could not cook without it.

"There is wood all over this town in piles!" the officer shouted. Could you not have picked it up?

"It was too far to carry," he said.

"We have no time for such as this. Now, be about your way and before you do, make your apologies to the owners."

The boy said the words, but Karalee could see he was angry.

When let go, he pulled his shirt back into place and slowly walked away; straight-backed and confident. Her heart went out to him. He was hardly past knee britches.

Dinner was *very* late and they talked at the dinner table only of the troubles that day. Classes didn't mix and yet every person was just that...a person. She excused herself and went upstairs, sat down in her room at the lovely desk and wrote a letter to Jackson on the family crested stationery.

The next thing Karalee knew, it was pitch dark. Workers, ordered to stop working at dusk so people could sleep, generally did as bidden, but tonight there was a bright light and the sounds of constant pounding and low voices.

She went to the window and could see the boy who had stolen the wood earlier picking up wood slats that the men were throwing off the top of a roof. One man helped the boy put some in a small wagon. When it was full he said a few words to the man who ruffled the boy's hair, then she watched as he headed down an alley.

She let the curtain fall back and smiled.

Sleep came sweet and easy that night. A letter waited on the desk for Jackson and time was passing so that soon, maybe in a month, she would be heading back to him.

Twenty

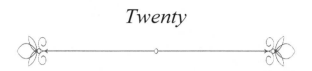

Karalee turned her calendar page. It was the first day of August. The City of Charleston had improved so much that she dared to think another few months, and with the warm southern temperatures, the town would be considerably livable.

Since it had taken them eight days to make the trip down, she would inquire to see if perhaps the rail lines in Atlanta had been improved enough so she could pick up the train there. She would make inquiries today.

Mother was much improved in her health and being among her former friends had given Karalee the hope she might return to Michigan by the first week of September. There would be time then before the snow came to pick up her life where she left off.

Except, and she hadn't thought of this, should Mother sign the house over to her? The deal with Mr. Rutledge had been forgotten in all the trouble. She had failed to find out where she stood. And somehow, someway, she was going to have to find a way to pay the taxes. Most of Father's money was gone.

Southerners were generally more laid back. She enjoyed the people, the weather and the food, become a fan of sweet tea and was a bit sad she would be leaving. She and Mother had not spoken a word about her going back. Karalee made it a point to find her and make arrangements to meet for an hour or two the minute she returned from a Ladies Meeting at St. Michael's Church. The building had been damaged but was still standing.

"Mother, I'm glad you are meeting with your lady friends. I'm sure you've gotten reacquainted with many of them."

"It's been good, Karalee," Mother said quietly. "I've actually found I enjoy them more than ever. I know it will be months before Charleston gains back the beauty she once had, but in the meantime, I need something to keep me busy. If you've noticed, I've not used the powders as much. I find that from the few blocks I walk each day to see the ladies, my leg fares better."

"I have noticed, Mother, but I didn't know you went to St. Michael's for your meetings. I assumed you were meeting at your friends' homes."

"Actually, we have been working on sewing children's clothes for Jameson's Orphanage. Those children are wretchedly poor," she said. "I must go. There's much to do, but I will look for you after dinner."

Karalee looked in her mother's eyes for a moment and smiled.

"I'm glad for you, Mama."

She watched while Mother, limping ever so slightly, made her way down the street. The way she walked, the way her eyes softened, had opened Karalee's eyes. Mother was where she was supposed to be. How had she suffered being in Michigan? Maybe she, her own daughter, had not understood just how much Mother longed for her childhood home.

Karalee was pondering those thoughts when it struck her. Jameson's Orphanage was for the poorest of the poor...all black children who had lost their parents. Mother was working for them.

* * *

As long as Mother had work to do, Karalee would be free to go. But before that happened, she had to know where she stood as far as the house. She could not live there alone. Even though Father had built it, she knew he wouldn't mind if she sold it. He would want it put to good use. All her memories were safe in her mind, and as long as she lived, she would never forget the house at 312 Broadway. Someone with a big family would be lovely there. She hated the thought, but the reality of life was so uncertain, she had learned nothing was safe from pain or loss. Karalee didn't want to live her life in fear and anger.

If Jackson asked her to marry him again, she would say yes. He would decide for her where she would live. All that mattered was they would be together. It had finally happened; Jackson had confessed all to her, which helped her understand his reluctance to marry—his fear of turning out like his father. Because he had openly faced his past, the pain of it had less power.

Smiling as she stepped outside, she sat on one of the white rockers, all six of them had made it down safely. Karalee ran her hand across the familiar wood. This is where they belonged. Right here on the oversized verandah, looking across the way to the Atlantic Ocean...where Mother wanted them to be. She couldn't be in Charleston before now, but she had stationed her beloved rockers on her Michigan verandah and tried to bring back her own memories.

Now she was living the life she had longed for. And Karalee knew it was good. One's heart could not un-love something when it longed for it. Father was never able to pluck the South out of his young bride's heart.

Life was hard. It was unfaithful at times, joyous beyond measure at others, and over in a few short years. One must make their way, if they were going to find any purpose. And it looked like Mother had found hers.

Karalee began a list of questions she would ask Mother tonight.

Dinnertime came before she knew it. She had napped in the heat of the day hoping to spend some evening time reading and making travel plans. It was a particularly hot first week of August.

Mother came in about four o'clock, declaring the women had had enough heat for one day, gone up to bathe and choose a lighter weight dress.

Karalee was out back waiting for Mother under the shade of a low hanging tree when she noticed the boy who had taken the wood. She peeked through a break in the bushes enclosing the yard. Only he wasn't alone. He had hold of a little girl's hand. She couldn't be above four years of age. Careful not to be staring, she followed inside the perimeter to see where they were going. Down the street was a fish market—downwind most times, thankfully, she had noted more than once on these hot days. They were heading that way.

Peering through the wood planked fence, she saw they were eating raw fish the man had tossed away. Immediately, without thinking, she opened the gate, gathered her skirts and marched down to the market.

"Sir, what is your price for boiled shrimp today?

He quoted her a price. Then she said, "Give these children as much as they wish and I will return with my payment."

"Yes, miss." He had seen this woman before. She was from the Drayton Manor. Hoity toity people, but what did it matter? He needed money to repair his dock that had been smashed by war ships.

The boy looked at her and remembering, felt ashamed and hurried away before she could return.

"Where is the boy?" Karalee recovered her breath after rushing back.

"They have left," he said, visibly disappointed.

She looked at him. "Will you give me your word, sir, than when they return, you will give them clean cooked fish, not the rotten fish? I will pay now and trust you will do the deed." She gave him the eye.

"I will, miss."

"Will you put that in writing please?" Father did not raise a fool.

He hesitated but did it. She turned over the money and walked away, eyes searching left and right...they had gone off hungry.

Suddenly, instead of returning home, she walked down this street and that street, then finally saw them sitting under a bush, not a tree, but a bush, seeking shelter from the sun.

Instead of approaching them, she hurried back to the house, asked Glory and the staff to quickly pack a large food basket with bread, fruit, meat and cheese.

Within minutes, they had done it. Karalee took the basket, smoothed the damp tendrils of hair back from her face and hoped she didn't look like a hooligan. On days like today one had enough to do to pull in a decent breath after a short walk. She set a smile on her face as she approached them slowly, her hand resting over her heart, anxious that they should not flee. She doubted she could catch them.

"I am so warm, do you mind if I sit with you?" she asked and they immediately scooted further down the railroad tie they were sitting upon.

She stared out at nothing and finally said, "I am very hungry, do you mind if I eat?"

They both shook their heads at once and she could see their eyes set deep in their skull, their wrists and ankles too thin.

She pulled out bread and took one bite, broke off two more pieces and handed some to them. They did not hesitate. Soon the three of them were eating a picnic lunch in a war-torn city with nothing but rubble around them. Karalee wanted to weep. Afraid to eat too much, she stopped and waited for them as they savored the food, then handed the basket to them, and said, "Take this to your mother."

The girl stared, the boy looked her in the eye and said, "We will miss. Thank you for your goodness."

"And I thank you for befriending me while I ate. It is too lonely to eat alone, yes?"

Two sets of eyes took her clue as she nodded. They nodded, too. "Now in a couple of days, if you would like to meet me here I shall need companionship. But only if you wish it," she added for good measure.

They were off, shoeless, dusty, and sweet. Her heart soared. She would write Jackson and tell him about the conditions here.

Rolling up her sleeves, she picked up her skirts and slowly walked home. Something must be done. And Mother's family could well afford to do it. She pressed her lips together and stopped by to remind the fish man that she would be asking the children if he kept his word.

He had pulled on his straw hat and nodded.

Mother was down from her bath, wondering where she had gotten off to. But when she said it, she wasn't angry.

"Shall we go out back? The sun will be setting soon and give us a bit of relief. "

"Have you eaten, Mother?"

"Yes, I was not so hungry so had ham and a biscuit. Have you?"

"Yes, I got some food from the kitchen."

"As you remember, Mother and Father are attending a wake. The banker. He lost everything and was not disposed to go on."

Karalee knew what that meant.

"Did he have a family?"

There's just his wife. She will go back to Connecticut."

"I'm sorry."

"As I am."

"Mother, would you tell me more about what you and the ladies are doing at St. Michael's?"

Mother turned to look at her daughter. "Yes, I can do that. We are sewing plain little dresses for the girls and pants for the boys. Another group of ladies from the Presbyterian Church are making shirts and skirts for them.

"How did you get started?"

"My friend, Leah, asked if I'd like to go, and I went."

"Just like that?"

"Just like that."

"The thing is, the dresses were so plain. I embroider a simple pattern around the bottom of each dress and hem it."

"Indeed. May I come with you one day?"

"If you wish."

Mother still answered curtly but Karalee could see tenderness in her eyes and her mannerism.

"We must do something. Perhaps I can help. I'm not near as good as you, but I can sew on buttons, if need be."

"We need buttons. Many have been saved from the people who have died, even the buttons off the soldier's uniforms have been collected. That was Leah's idea. She said that there had been so much loss, that every single thing that could help the living was worth the doing."

Karalee felt her eyes burn.

She and Mother were of the same mind.

Twenty-One

The last few days passed in absolute complicity with Mother. It was time she had the conversation with Mother as to what she wanted to do with the house.

The judge had ordered Mr. Rutledge to turn Mother's house back to the owner, further that he and mother have no future contact. Under no circumstances were they to see each other or make any contracts or agreements between them.

Both agreed and that was the end of it, so Mother had the house back along with the balance on the mortgage, which Karalee knew happened to be upwards of four thousand dollars—more than she could make in three years if she had a position.

"How can you ever hope to keep the house, Karalee, if you don't marry?"

"If I cannot find a position, I will marry."

"Who? There are few gentleman left in Cassopolis. You had excellent choices two years ago."

She could hear Mother's former tone of voice returning and decided to settle the matter.

"If Jackson Woodridge asks me again, I *will* marry him."

Mother huffed.

A person couldn't be expected to change overnight, Karalee reminded herself.

"Well, then at least you will have a roof over your head and food at your table. But be reminded that you will also gain a child that is not your own."

"I know, Mother. I don't mind." She wondered how Mama knew about Jackson's son. A reminder jumped in her head: the ladies at the tea party.

"Whatever life he had before you knew him, produced that child. You will have to live with that."

Karalee forced her voice to stay calm. "That is true. And I am willing. More than willing."

"Then you have made up your mind?"

"Yes, I have, which is what I wanted to talk to you about. I want to start home by the first week of September so that I can help with the harvesting."

"Unmarried, and yet you will be down there with him harvesting?"

Mother clicked her tongue. "I didn't say that. I'll stay at Lily's house, but I intend to help. If he doesn't ask me to marry him, I will force him."

"Karalee Elizabeth, no daughter of mine will go begging for a husband!"

"I was being facetious, Mother." She laughed a little, happy that they were actually sharing a light moment—at least on her part. "So then it is settled. I will sell the house. We will split the money?"

When her mother hesitated, Karalee thought that perhaps she had been a bit forward in her assumption.

"No. That will not do. You will keep the money. If you marry you may keep my half as your wedding gift, if not, you may want to keep the house in hopes you will find a husband before the money runs out."

"I hadn't thought of that. Good point. It is settled then?"

Mother nodded her agreement.

"Thank you Mother. I shall keep yours and Father's house in the family."

Without acknowledgement, Mother continued.

"I will have the papers drawn. When Grandaddy and Granmama pass on, the Charleston house and Magnolia Breeze will be mine. Magnolia Breeze will have to be sold. I cannot run the plantation. I am to understand the house has been saved because it was used as a hospital. The crops have been burned and are in a state of ruination. But it will bring me cash enough to save Drayton Manor."

Suddenly, Mother changed the topic. "It is unfortunate that Samuel lost his life and Henderson has never returned home."

"Yes, it is." Karalee agreed. Samuel died, not in the war, but in a terrible tornado in Atlanta just months before the Civil War started.

His entire family was lost. "And Henderson was never interested in the house or the plantation. He was a wild and willful soul."

"I have no need of money," she declared.

"I know, Mother. You have been blessed." She kept her voice kind. "And for that I am grateful. You will be all right."

"But we will not be together."

Karalee thought that an odd statement. "No, Mother, we will not be together. Your heart is here and mine is with Jackson, if he will have me."

"If that kiss you two snuck at the train depot was any sign, I don't think you have to worry," she said dryly.

"You saw that?" Karalee felt her already warm face, burn hotter.

"I'm not blind, you know."

Karalee chuckled.

"I remember when your Father kissed me like that...I ended up in Michigan."

Now they both laughed. Karalee teared up at once. "Then you *did* love Father when you married?"

"Of course I did. What made you think otherwise?"

Karalee pressed her fingers to her lips. "I'm glad you loved Father," she said simply.

Mother did love Father. The thought curbed some of the pent-up memories when she wondered if Mother ever did. Karalee couldn't wipe the satisfied smile from her face. They were talking like mother and daughter, not enemies.

A dog barked loudly nearby and interrupted their reverie. Mother stood with the help of her cane and walked away slowly, then turned and called over her shoulder, "The ladies meet again tomorrow at eight o'clock. Later, now that the hot weather has arrived."

"I'll be ready."

Karalee took a short walk to see if the two children were about. Three days had passed. She had looked every day, meandering and hoping to see them before their food ran out.

On the fourth day, she found them. They smiled shyly but made no move to leave the railroad tie under the shade of the large bush.

"Good morning," she greeted them with a smile and sat down at the far end of their seat. "I was wondering if I might ask you a question." She looked to the boy.

"I have some books I think you might like."

"I can read," the boy said proudly. "Mama taught me. My sister is too small, but I'm going to teach her."

"Good for you. My goodness, we don't even know each other's name," she exclaimed. "My name is Karalee."

"I'm Hayward. And this is Judith."

"Very nice to make your acquaintance," Hayward nodded.

Karalee noted his pride as he spoke like a southern gentleman. "As it is you see, I have no children. And find that I must have something to do. Would you like me to read this story?" She pulled out a book from the bag she had brought along.

"Yes, please. I want Judith to see more books. She had only one and it is gone with ..." He shrugged.

With slow movements, Karalee scooted just a bit closer and began to read, waiting for them to devour the words and the colorful scenes before she turned the pages. "Hayward, why don't you read the last few lines for your sister?"

He looked at her for a long moment and took the book, turned the page and began to read slowly, his index finger moving along the page.

Karalee couldn't help it. Her eyes filled with tears. Judith was wide-eyed and Hayward proud. Overwhelming emotions churned inside.

"Well, wasn't that nice? Perhaps we can meet tomorrow, if your mother and father say it is all right."

"Our father is gone and Mama has lung fever."

"May I ask if your mama is home?"

"No, she can't be with us. We might catch what she has. She's with the sisters in the convent way up on the hill. If she gets better she can come home."

"I am famished. Might it be okay with your mama, do you think, if you joined me for supper? "

Hayward looked at his sister with concern. "Yes, I think it will be all right."

Karalee let out a breath. "Fine, then you shall be my guests." She stood. "We live in that house." She pointed. "Just a short walk away."

Hayward stood and said, "I cannot go there. I took wood from them without asking and the officer said I must stay away."

"I know about that, Hayward. It was a mistake. Should the officer come by, I will tell him you are my guest."

He didn't look convinced.

"What of the man who owns the house? Might not he be angry at me?"

"He is my Grandaddy and he will not be angry. I will see to it."

Hayward hesitated and kicked at the dirt with his bare toe, looked at his sister again and said, "Yes, we will come."

Karalee breathed again.

"Excellent! Let me think. I do believe we are having chicken and potatoes this evening." Two pairs of eyes widened. "Come, Hayward, we will tell the kitchen staff we have two guests for dinner, and then you can help me find a book from the library for your sister."

Karalee, glad her grandparents were not home, hurried the children upstairs and had the servants prepare a warm bath for each. At least they would be presentable should her family walk in.

The staff allowed her to let them eat their dinner early, being informed there was enough to go around. The elder couple didn't eat much, the cook said. Karalee sensed the cook also knew her grandparents would be horrified at barefoot waifs in their house, much less sitting at their elegant dining room table.

"Thank you so much. We will try to be done and out of the way early."

"Don't you worry none, Miss Karalee. We be quick. We know our duties 'round here."

"Mother is upstairs, resting. She will wait to be called when Grandaddy and Granmama sit down for dinner. We will be gone by then."

"Yes, miss."

Karalee wanted to tell her she did not have to address her as such, but kept her thoughts to herself. This was the way of the Southern people. She need not meddle.

The children were groomed with help from Glory, and positioned at the large table along with Karalee. When the food was set before them, the children had the look of hunger.

"Shall we begin?" Karalee said a quick prayer and picked up her fork. Two sets of large eyes watched her. They picked up their fork and leaned over the plates, and started to shovel food in their mouths.

"Please slow down children. You will make yourselves ill. There is more."

Karalee wondered if she were harsh and knew by their looks, they were not offended. They both began to relax. Probably used to grabbing food and running, they were now free to eat without fear of being seized.

Hayward had some food left on his plate and he poked Judith's arm and whispered for her to save some.

She complied, immediately setting her fork down, her very clean hands looked so small. She wondered that Hayward, a nine-year-old, could be in charge of a young child. They were older than their age, Karalee could only assume. Living alone, finding food and shelter. She felt an instant shot of anger rush through her body.

"Children, I will be back. Don't worry. I'm going to the kitchen. Would you like more milk?"

Judith looked to her brother. He nodded.

"Glory," Karalee called out. Glory appeared instantly. "Somethin' be wrong miss?"

"Yes, there is!" She noted Glory's eyes grew large, her countenance afraid.

"There are children starving in this community! Would you please see to it that Hayward and Judith have food any time they knock at the door out back? I will pay for it, if necessary."

"Miss Williams, ya best be speakin' to Cook 'bout that. I ain't got no say-so."

Karalee nodded. "I'm sorry Glory. I'm not angry with *you*."

"I knows dat Miss Williams, you mad 'cause dos kids ain't got food."

Karalee could have hugged her. In fact, she did. "Where is Cook?"

"She be outside stayin' cool while y'all eat."

"Thank you." Karalee marched out the door and pulled the afternoon air into her lungs...it was thick with mist. She calmed herself and tried to breathe.

"Cook, the meal is very good. I want to ask you to favor me with your time if you can."

Cook stood up quickly. "Course, miss." Her eyes were large with fear, too.

"I'm wondering, if it doesn't cause you trouble, if you would give any extra food you may have to Hayward and Judith if I send them to your door in the evenings?"

"I be checkin' with Mr. and Mrs. Drayton. Dey might not allow dat."

"I see." Karalee nodded. "Then I will take it up with them. But tonight if you would be so kind as to make a small basket for them, I will answer to Grandaddy and Granmama if they should call you out."

"Yes, miss," she said with a smile. "I be obliged to do dat for ya."

"I have not even asked your name. I know it is not Cook," she said, delighted to have someone on her side.

"My name is Philomena Williams."

"Miss Philomena, I hope we will be friends. We share a last name." She shook the Cook's hand and dashed away.

Philomena chuckled aloud and went back to work. "Well, a Yankee she be, but a pretty nice one, to my way o'thinkin'." On the way, Philomena snatched two carrots and two apples from the cool house.

"Now, if you are ready, we will carry our plates to Miss Philomena and she will save the rest of your food, while we go look at books," Karalee instructed.

That was done and all signs that they had eaten at the table were gone. Pleased, she led them to Grandaddy's library. She kept her ear sharpened to any noise of clip-clopping horses on the cobblestones out front.

The afternoon had fallen away. "You must take your books and get home before dark," Karalee warned them. "I will come with you and carry your plates, see you are safe and come back myself."

Hayward gave her a look. "You don't need to come, Miss Karalee." He was now allowed to call her by her given name. "We will be safe."

Karalee knew Hayward was head of his house and let them go at the corner behind Drayton Manor. Reluctantly, she returned. They had extra carrots and apples, thanks to Philomena who had bought them at the market for herself, and two books to read.

Back to the kitchen. "Philomena, please do not put your job in jeopardy. If you are unable to assist the children, I will gather the food myself and take it to them."

"Miss Williams...."

Karalee interrupted. "Please, call me Karalee."

"Miss Karalee..." she began again, "I be seein' to it. If there is any trouble I be comin' to you."

"Thanks, my friend." She hugged a very stiff Philomena and knocked her white hat sideways on her head in the doing of it.

"You be a Yankee, but you be a good woman." She chuckled as she walked away, straightening her hat.

Karalee felt alive. There was so much work to be done here. People were coming from the countryside to help rebuild Charleston to its former glory. This was the least they could do. Even Mother had pitched in to help the children at the orphanage. She and Karalee had become totally involved.

Life needed purpose, she realized later as she was sewing buttons on the backs of Mother's embroidered dresses. She was proud of her. Mama was home.

Twenty-Two

The days passed too quickly. Karalee had hoped to leave but it seemed she could not pull away from Mama, and what would Hayward and Judith do after she left?

Grandaddy and Granmama were unaware of much unless it concerned them directly. No wonder Mama had such high expectations put on her. They still treated her like she was their young daughter instead of a widow with grown children.

And the odd thing was Mother didn't seem to mind. Karalee wondered if she'd always needed their approval. And now she had it. Would the world never cease to be free of broken people? Rich or poor? Good or evil? She doubted it very much.

The people of Charleston were overworked, tired, and hungry. Thankfully, Grandaddy insisted they at least donate some of their cash to the people who were helping rebuild, and two times a month he donated money to feed those who were working on the streets to repair and reconstruct their city. Karalee was proud of him, especially because Granmama had not wanted to part with the money.

She watched one evening as Grandaddy and Mother were sitting in the lush parlor discussing the kids at the orphanage. Seems Grandaddy was not as harsh as she had thought. He handed Mama a few bills and told her to get fabric to make those kids some decent clothes. Then a bit more… to buy shoes *if* they could find any to be bought.

Each step up the wide curved staircase was an effort; there were twenty-two of them, she and John had counted. Tired tears were ready to spill. First for the citizens of Charleston, then for the fact she was able to help two children while their mother was ill, and third because she had a heart full of joy. Mother was home. She could hardly wait to soak in a warm bath and then crawl into a clean, soft bed. It was the best kind of tired she had ever felt.

* * *

The days marched forward. Two letters had arrived from Jackson in one thick envelope. Lily had tucked a missive in with her brother's. She went out and sat in a rocker and read. She saved Lily's letter for last. Jackson wrote he had a great crop of corn and James was a good help. He sounded so happy. Karalee missed his deep voice... wanted to be in his strong arms again, and share a kiss. He had branded her with *that kiss* at the train depot. Her heart was torn in halves: North and South.

Heart beating fast, she opened Lily's note. She had met a gentleman, a former Union officer who had come home to find his wife had died in childbirth just three months before he arrived. He had been distraught from the war, had walked in the door of his wife's parents' house where she had been staying, then learned she and the girl child were gone. He left to grieve for several months, and had finally returned home.

Lily met him at the General Store after he knocked a full basket of eggs to the floor with a rake he had just picked up. She had bent down along with him to clean up the mess and when he raised his eyes to apologize, she saw the eyes of a man who was broken. He had cleaned the floor, not smiling once, and then they stood, her hands dripping with slimy eggs off the ends of her fingertips. So he had called the owner from the back and ordered him to bring a wet towel.

She had smiled and said, "Still issuing orders?" Lily hoped he wasn't offended.

"Seventh Calvary," he admitted.

They had talked a minute, but he was anxious to be left alone.

"As God would have it," Lily wrote, "Jackson brought him by the house for supper one night. He mentioned he'd hired a man."

Karalee laughed out loud. "God, indeed," she whispered and tapping her toe to the floor, rocked mama's chair and read more. The sun was going down so she hurried through the letter.

The man had come home too late to plant a crop so was looking for something to do until spring. Jackson had needed the help and so he became part of the family. He had given him room and board so they could take turns harvesting the fields and taking care of the animals.

She made it through the letter just as her eyes were straining to see the last words and gasped. "This is all?"

Lily gave no clue about the man, not even his name? Karalee had to read back through again. "Peter Bond," she said aloud. She was excited, for Lily had been her brother's keeper. Perhaps she would find some happiness herself.

Karalee stood, held the letters to her bosom and prayed, "God lead me and Lily and Jackson, Grandaddy, Granmama, Mama, Philomena and especially Hayward and Judith." She rushed up the stairs with great strength and began to lay clothes on the bed. She wanted to go home. The fields would be done, but it was okay she was leaving a little late. It would give Jackson time to enjoy the autumn weather. She would have to look for a position, too. The taxes were always waiting. Anxious to be about her trip, she checked the calendar. It was the twenty-third of August. Karalee had no idea it was this late in the month. "I must tell Mama I'm leaving. She has work now and it will be easier," she thought aloud. Hayward and Judith had a home to stay in... Philomena had taken them to her house. Her children had grown and left, and her man died.

Folks frowned at a black woman taking in two white children, but Philomena didn't care. "God don't see no color," she had said firmly, which brought tears to Karalee. They were safe. Then she asked Grandaddy, when they were alone, if he would help Philomena take care of the children. He had frowned at first, it was outside his beliefs, seeing black folks only as servants rather than people, but finally agreed.

She was free to be on her way. What a joyous evening! Glory brought hot water for her bath and Karalee let her wash her long, thick hair and comb it out. It had become a wonderful ritual. Stations in life were always present, but Karalee had seen them dissolve as hearts were drawn together, regardless of color, position or money. It had been good for her to come. *God you knew that didn't you? I needed to see people working together. I have a feel now for what Southerners were facing. I just wish we could have handled it without all the destruction of lives and property, but then again, I imagine you wished that from the first.* She sighed as Glory finished her hair.

"Glory. Please sit down." Karalee patted the chair next to her and watched as Glory, a quick gaze at the door, sat down.

"Miss?"

"Would you mind carrying up more water, Glory?"

"Whatever' fo miss? You already be clean."

"Would you like a bath? A warm bath and let me do your hair?"

"Oh, miss, you done lost your mind." She laughed standing to her feet.

"I mean it," Karalee said quietly. "I'll let the water drain and you can bring fresh. I'll bring you towels."

"Now, I knows you be Yankee, miss. I can't use dat bathroom o' yours."

"You can if I say so."

"And what 'bout if yo Grandaddy finds out?" Glory's hands were on her hips now.

"He won't."

"No, I ain't takin' no chance. I gotta tin tub at home dat cleans me jus' fine."

"I'm letting the water out. You'd better be up here with that hot water."

"You orderin' me?"

"Yes. I am."

Glory shook her head and did her bidding.

Karalee heard her low chuckle as she descended the back service stairs.

"Now, doesn't that feel good? You can soak as long as you like. I'm going to pack a few things. The door is locked so no one will come in."

"Dey gonna smell me and knows I be in your bath." She laughed from the other room.

It was Karalee's turn to chuckle.

"I be out der in a minute and help ya pack. Leastways, I can tell ev'ybody what I be doin' up here so long."

"Okay. But let me comb out your hair first."

"Miss Karalee, you shore gonna cause me trouble if ya don't watch out," she said standing in the doorway, the huge towel wrapped around her.

"Good. Sit here. Your hair is so long. Doesn't it get hot?"

109

"Yeah, but well, my man, he be likin'it long," she said shyly.

"I didn't know you were married."

"Just six months." She planted her hands in her lap. "Com' on now, I can't be sittin' here all day."

Karalee got to work. "Okay, now show me how you wind it up like you do."

Glory showed her. Karalee stuck pins everywhere to hold it up, and Glory got back into her clothes. "I gotta get movin'. I be so relaxed I might just fall 'sleep standin' up."

An hour later, the two had laid out several stacks of clothing. Karalee resolved she was only taking one trunk back. She hated above all things to carry too much baggage when one needed so little to get by.

"I'll be down for dinner," Karalee said as Glory slipped out the door. She could hear her fast footsteps as she hurried down the hall.

Grandaddy and Granmama were attending a play at the theatre. It was the least damaged building so was repaired first so workers and families could have a bit of entertainment. It was opening night.

So it was just her and Mama for dinner.

Karalee went to the kitchen and saw Glory was not there. She had probably been given another duty somewhere in the house. Soon enough, Glory appeared bringing dishes from the afternoon tea and as soon as she walked past Philomena, there was dead silence.

Philomena looked at her, "Girl, you smell like Miss Karalee's rose water when ya sashayed by me. You be upstairs in her room?" she accused, sudsy hands resting on her hips.

Staying out of sight, Karalee slapped a hand over her mouth. She saw Glory whisper in Philomena's ear.

"Ya don't say?" Philomena's brown eyes huge. "Well, dat don't surprise me none! Ya say she made ya do it?"

"Yep. She ordered me ta take dat bath."

Karalee slipped away. She loved these two women.

Twenty-Three

Karalee was fully packed by the last week of August and had only a small satchel to keep a few necessary items close by. Mama was moody at the last ladies meeting when she announced her daughter would soon be returning to Michigan, much to everyone's disappointment.

She was due to leave the second day of September, had informed Jackson via mail she would cable when she arrived in Atlanta and to expect delays. The electric lines were still down around Charleston. Fortunately, mail went out once a week now and trickled in at the same pace. She sent the letter three days ago. It would give him time to plan for her arrival. There was a long journey ahead and this time she would be traveling alone.

Her grandparents were sad to see her go, but knew all children and grandchildren had to live their own lives, and Karalee suspected, they wanted the quietness of their home back.

The moment she dreaded most was saying goodbye to Hayward and Judith. She would be spending as much time as possible with them while Philomena was at work.

The days were roaring hot so she wore light-weight dresses, two that her grandmother insisted she take back home. Karalee loved them: one, a cotton rose-colored flower print against a soft green background, and the other, a soft yellow and light blue plaid with a wide blue ruffle at the bottom. She had picked out the fabrics and the designs, and then Granmama's best seamstress had sewn them up.

Finally, it all wound down. It was the last day of August. She had made the rounds with her new friends...just two more days left in Charleston. It was a particularly warm and humid day; the ladies' meeting at the church had been called off. The church was too hot after being shut up during the week.

Mama had gone down the road to meet with a few of her new friends. They were working on a quilt to give to the children at the orphanage. Mother had almost decided not to go, then at the last minute realized she'd be just as hot laying across her bed up on the second floor as she would be sitting in the parlor of Mrs. Dean's house, talking and whiling away the time until relief came in the evening.

When Mother came home, she went to the kitchen, poured herself a large glass of sweet tea and carried it up the stairs. "I'm going to bed early tonight."

"Sleep well, Mother. It's only seven-thirty. Hopefully, you'll get some rest."

Her mother stopped midway up the stairs, one hand on the rail, the other carrying the glass of tea, and looked back. "You best get some rest, too…you'll be worn out before you start home."

"I will Mother." Karalee waited with bated breath, as she watched her take each step with a slight wince. It was still hard for her to put weight on the injured leg. Doc told her not to help unless absolutely necessary—*patients did not heal who did not work for it themselves*. He was right. She could see Mother had made it on her own.

Satisfied she was doing the right thing, Karalee took a book to the library. Suddenly she knew it would be harder to leave Mama than she had thought. There was a slow-moving fan in that room. She pulled the curtains closed against the heat of the day and turned on a light. It was after nine o'clock by the time she thought about heading to bed.

She made a quick trip to the kitchen for a glass of water, and had just put her foot on the bottom step of the stairs when she felt something beneath her feet. The floor seemed like water, then the house began to shake, and she heard noises outdoors like she'd never heard before—bricks tumbling, rocks crushing against each other, trees cracking and crashing to the earth. Was it a hurricane? The clouds had not been dark. Her glass fell to the stone floor and shattered. She held onto the railing. The house was going to fall down upon her, she could feel it. Mirrors crashed and scattered, tables overturned with Granmama's beautiful glass vases exploding, spilling water and flowers. Then the huge crystal chandelier began swaying and in one fell swoop, fell to the floor and splintered into a million pieces. Karalee covered her eyes against the shattering glass and clung to the rail which seemed as though it would be torn from her hands. Surely they were all going to perish. After what seemed like forever... the shaking stopped.

Then the screaming began. She rushed to the door, avoiding the glass as much as she could—glad she still had her shoes. She stood in the doorway. The ground was dry. There was no rain and there had been no warning of bad weather. She tried to reason, but the screams of people needing help pounded in her head. She saw a small child wandering mindlessly in the street as people began to come out of the ruins in their night clothes.

Her eyes did not fool her. The town was in shambles. Again. "Oh God, has this city the cover of death over it?" she said aloud. "Please God, help."

Mama! Karalee turned and found her way back to the stairs; the house was dark. She reached out until she found and grabbed the railing and forced her weak legs to climb. What of Grandaddy and Granmama upstairs in their bed?

She heard Mother's groans and tried to open her door, but it wouldn't budge. The framing had changed positions. "Mama, I'm here. Are you injured?"

"No...I am able to walk. I was thrown from my bed, but I am safe. Go check on Grandaddy and Granmama," she ordered.

Karalee tried to kick her way through the debris, finally lifted her dress up and over her head and rid herself of it. The dust nearly smothered her as she tossed it aside.

The door to her grandparents' room was wide open. Karalee felt a chill. There were no voices. It was almost as if it was open so their souls could walk through. She shook her head and feared the worst. What make her think of such a thing?

Blackness filled the room. There were no gas lamps from outside to light the windows.

She heard Mother shouting from down the hall or was it someone from below stairs. She stopped and listened. A man was calling. He was holding a candle and coming up the stairs yelling, "Anyone hurt! Anyone hurt?"

"Here," Karalee answered and coughed dust out of her lungs. The eerie light coming up the stairs signaled he had reached the top when the hallway lit up. She couldn't believe she'd made it through that mess.

"Mother, someone is here. We'll check and be back to get you," she shouted hoarsely.

"Don't worry. See about your grandparents," she hollered back.

"Here," Karalee's voice guided the man's light her way. "Careful of the glass," she cautioned.

He was in trousers and undershirt, was dusty head to foot, and had a few abrasions about his face and arms. She reached out in front of the blackness and felt for the doorway. He lifted the light.

They were in their bed. He drew closer. They were under the coverlet. She could see their forms. He bravely and slowly pulled back the coverlet as glass and splinters fell away. They were huddled together, dust covering them. Dust to dust. Karalee thought irrationally. She wanted to scream. There was nothing to do. They were gone. She felt for a moment that her legs would give out. Grandaddy's spectacles lay across the room, crushed, fallen from the table he laid them on every night.

"We mustn't let on," she whispered and clamped a hand over her mouth. The man held up the light and she could see the dread in him, as well. "Is anyone else in the house?"

"Just Mama. I need help opening her door."

He held the candle high as they made their way and he pushed his shoulder into the door until it opened. He checked to see if Mother was okay, and then Karalee told him to go. The screaming and yelling grew louder in the streets. "You're needed elsewhere." She coughed again. "Thank you. We will manage now."

"There will be aftershocks. Leave them here, he nodded toward the other bedroom, and you two get downstairs and stand in the doorway when the next one comes. Away from windows if you can, or things hanging above…if there is anything left hanging," he added.

He held up the light until he saw her and Mother coming out of the room, then led the way.

Once they were safely down, he stepped over the debris and hurried through the front door, which was now hanging at odd angles.

"They're gone aren't they? Mother and Father?"

"Yes," Karalee said softly, then…"Hurry Mother, I feel the floor beginning to tremble again. They stood in the front doorway, thankful the beautiful crystal chandelier from above was now in shards around them. Karalee thought what a crazy idea *that* was. It was Granmama's favorite piece in the entire house. But it didn't matter now. She stood in her underskirts in shock. It felt like the world had ended…for some it already had. She couldn't even cry.

She and Mama held on while the first aftershock came…seeing the huge pillars tremble out front made her sick. If those gave way, they would be crushed. But she stayed, closed her eyes and prayed God would save them. When the moving ended, Karalee opened her eyes again. Had everyone who was left survived this one? She heard bricks crumbling to the ground and glass breaking, but not like the first time. They were still alive.

Twenty-Four

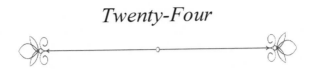

Karalee and Mother sat out on the verandah, afraid to go back inside. At the first sign of light, the people were standing in the streets. A farmer's wagon drove slowly through town. Someone had put black fabric on the sideboards. It stopped as people waved it down and a body was added, then another and another.

When it rattled near, Karalee wrapped herself in a dusty blanket and stood out on the street out front and waved for it to stop. Two men tipped their hats and followed her up the stairs. She looked and Mother had gone. Tears falling down her dusty face, Karalee stood alone on the front verandah of the once beautiful mansion and watched in disbelief as Grandaddy and Granmama were carried down in blankets and laid next to each other in the wagon. It moved on down the street. She could see someone else waving for it to stop.

There was nothing that could be done. Karalee could not watch anymore, let Mother grieve alone wherever she had gone, and went inside to see what could be salvaged. Cries could be heard in the eerily quiet morning when someone else expired. She knew the haunting sound would never leave her. A woman walked by alone with a child in her arms who looked to be four or five. She refused to put the little boy in the wagon…simply walked behind it.

Trees were uprooted, and chimneys lay in heaps beside homes. Telegraph poles and wires were strewn about. People were afraid to go inside and started making small tents from rope and blankets in White Point Park and any other open space that was safe from falling buildings.

People salvaged whatever they could from their homes to make do. Karalee carried two mattresses with the help of others, and then made a tent beneath a tree so Mother could rest. Next, she went looking for Hayward and Judith. Philomena's house, a wood structure, was completely collapsed. There was no sign of them. She asked anyone walking by if they had seen her or the children, but few heard Karalee's voice. They were in a state of shock, all fending for themselves.

Two days later she had news. The three had gone up the way to Philomena's brother's house in Summerville and all were safe.

Karalee threw herself into doing whatever needed to be done. Two strong young men carried Granmama's sofas and the two matching chairs, purchased from Paris, out to their site. At least someone could sit on them instead of the hard ground. Others followed her idea. Children were sent out to gather branches from the downed trees. Every camp had plenty of wood to make fires for cooking, washing, or the slim chance of a chilly evening.

There were several campsites around the city, each trying to survive. The rich alongside the poor, making do. Council members met under trees and sent riders to surrounding cities to bring people who could help. Each day wagons came with supplies: food, water, rakes, saws and tools to begin the clean-up. Work horses pulled wagonloads of broken bricks that were then dumped in the lowlands.

Soon more wagons came with men, boys, and women with medical skills came along to set arms or legs that had been broken, and help with mothers who were expecting babies.

Three weeks passed. Karalee hardly had time to think. Mother kept busy cleaning the campsite, while she went to help whoever needed assistance and did what she could.

Today someone had brought in handmade rakes and brooms. Mother swept dirt off the bed sheet, which served as a floor.

"The wind is blowing it back inside," she complained, then gave up and put water on to boil. They had made a cupboard of sorts from wood planks and bricks, and on one shelf Mama's best tea cup sat with a small container of sugar nearby. A pot was at the ready and a small fire.

Karalee gazed sadly as she returned to their place and saw her mother sitting in Granmama's beautiful chair sipping tea from her best cup, her hair pulled back tight, away from her face.

"Where were you? I made tea." She gestured with a swing of her hand.

"I'll make mine," Karalee said tiredly and dropped into the other chair.

"We have enough to do around here without you going all up and down the street. You mustn't wear yourself out."

"Mother, what else am I to do? I'd rather work. The day goes faster and Mrs. Bonhoeffer needs help with her two little ones, just having the new baby."

"Karalee, why must you be everyone's savior?"

"Why must you ask me that, Mother?" She felt a tired smile creep onto her face, tight with sunburn after days outdoors.

"Put on a hat, at least. No man will want a woman with skin as dark as yours."

"Mother, no one cares about skin. Besides I'll never have the milky white skin you were born with."

Weather seemed to be against them, as well. Nights were burning, bugs swarming in one's face day *and* night, and children crying from the heat. Some folks took to drinking and others played card games in the slightly cooler parts of the early evening, before the sun went down. After that, there was mostly the buzz of quiet talk.

Soon wagons were coming more often. Word had finally reached outlying cities. Those homes with less damage hauled in new lumber for rebuilding. Boys and girls were assigned the job of cleaning bricks so they could be used again, plus picking up trash and keeping the fires burning.

More help meant more men to feed. Karalee had a few of the boys carry out Granmama's huge black cauldron and someone made a triangle stand. It fit perfectly over the fire. She stirred ham from the storehouses with beans for the men. Makeshift tables made with wood planks and bricks were set all around. Some folks made cornbread in their iron pots and others managed to make pots of soup.

That night after the men had been fed and had bedded down for the night, Karalee washed the dust off her face and settled on the pallet she had in the tent and slept. Even the sounds of the men snoring or children crying didn't reach her ears.

As dawn crept up, early risers quietly made their way to the latrine, such as it was: any old outhouses that were still standing were lined up in the woods. Men to the south, women to the north. There were already footpaths from the many visitors. Karalee made her trip and then decided she would rake the area. The sticks could be used for kindling and truth was, her shoes were so thin, she was tired of sticks poking through.

Finally the wagons stopped going to the graveyard just out of town. People were surviving and doing a good job of it, Karalee thought as she worked. By late afternoon, she felt light-headed and sat down under a low hanging tree, out of the late September sun and rested, then rose up again and kept raking. The wind was blowing and dust was flying. She hadn't had water in a while, and was about ready to head to their tent when she heard a new batch of wagons coming from a different direction. More help. She'd finish here and head up to assist with the cooking.

Loud shouts from the people welcomed the men and everything they had brought along. She could hear them mention books, medicine, potatoes, carrots, bags of beans and rice. Life would go on.

Feeling lightheaded again, she felt her ears ring. Shouts came across the wind. She thought she heard her name, stopped and leaned on the rake. Just the wind. Then she heard it again. Mother? She listened more closely. She knew no one else with her name and then realized it was a man's voice. Who would be calling her?

She turned and saw someone running toward her and squinted, her hand above her brow to defuse the sun.

"Karalee!"

The rake fell from her hands. "Jackson?"

She knew that hat. In an instant, she felt life return but could not make her feet move. She hoped she was not imagining things and blinked. Then he had his arms around her, her skirts swinging outward. When he set her on her feet, she felt her knees buckle, and then she was being lifted.

"Karalee," he whispered in her ear. "I found you."

"Jackson," she said with a hoarse voice from the constant raising of dust.

"You are safe."

"Yes. Mama and I are both safe."

Twenty-Five

At her direction, Jackson carried Karalee to their tent and put her on the sofa. "Lie down. You are spent," he said.

"I cannot lie down. There's too much to be done," she said and started to get up.

"I'll do what you need done."

"Don't leave just yet," she begged, too tired to sit up.

Jackson pulled up a wooden chair and sat next to her, relaxed, ankle over his knee. "Tell me all."

Karalee didn't want him to leave, his gaze as hungry as hers. "Your hair is longer," she whispered with a smile.

"There was no one to cut it for."

When she saw the love in his eyes, tears started to fall. Thick, heavy tears.

Jackson stayed where he was instead of hauling her into his arms. He knew Karalee would not like the public display of affection, so he spoke softly.

"What were you doing when I arrived?"

"Raking branches together for kindling," She managed to control herself by sheer force, having learned as a young girl not to display one's emotions in public.

"I'll take over. You stay here and rest. When I come back, I'll be hungry." He stood and punched on his hat. "I won't be back for a few hours. I'm tired of sitting in that wagon," he said with a wink.

Karalee watched him walk away and felt her eyelids close. She was safe. Jackson was here.

* * *

Sometime later Karalee felt the ache in her back when she tried to move and wiped spittle from the corner of her mouth. Someone had made a sort of canopy over her and the shade had kept the sun from burning her eyes.

Slowly, she forced herself to move, after a delightful rest. Then she remembered. Jackson was here!

Mother walked into their camp. "Jackson and I have been talking," she said in her matter-of-fact way. "He will be staying here with us."

Karalee stretched her legs and nodded.

"I'm making cornbread. You might want to make some soup. We have three potatoes, three carrots and a nice chunk of beef."

"Indeed?" Karalee thought their meat was gone.

"From one of the wagons. It was our camp's turn to get some vittles."

Karalee smiled noting her mother was talking in her Southern way. She got up and washed her hands with as little water as possible. How are we on water?"

"A new bucket for us right there." Mother pointed.

"I'll prepare the potatoes and carrots."

Within an hour the soup, which filled hardly more than the bottom of the huge cauldron, was bubbling nicely over the fire. The cornbread was just done. "I'll go for Jackson."

"Stay put. He told me he'd be here in a bit. No sense wasting yourself. You were doing too much, Karalee Elizabeth."

Karalee took off her apron and tried to smooth her hair and realized it was the best she could do. No one was putting on airs. No one had the time. Every family was touched by some grief or loss. She paced and tried not to look in the area where she thought he may be working. He would come when he came.

It was nearing dusk and everyone tried to have supper and dishes done before the sun set. Early rising was required. Everyone worked by daylight.

"Here he comes," Mother said calmly.

Karalee felt her heart beat faster. She had never seen anything more beautiful than his face earlier that morning as he walked right up to her. His arms tight around her waist had been so comforting, Karalee wanted to weep when he let her go. She watched him pull off his hat and snap it against his pants, dust raising and blowing behind him. Then he shoved his work worn hand through his hair, his beautiful dark hair, and she knew one thing: He was *her* man.

* * *

When Jackson saw her standing there, a slow smile crept across his face. He would never leave her again. There were things to be worked out with her mother, and he would see to it. Not tonight. But tomorrow, for certain.

* * *

Mother and Karalee sat down to a makeshift table with two tree stumps for seats. Jackson had walked over to the next camp and asked to borrow one of their stumps, returned, and joined them.

Then Mother served in Granmama's best dishes. They ate in silence. Karalee couldn't help but look away from Jackson's gaze. She also knew her mother was astute—probably noting every look that passed between them.

Twice Jackson handed her something and she felt his hand press hers, lingering.

Suddenly Mother jumped up and said, "I'm going to visit Mrs. Bonhoeffer. You two clean up here," she said and was gone.

"Hmmm..." Karalee said. "It's not like her to leave the dishes about."

"I asked her to give us time to talk."

"And she agreed?"

Jackson gave her a look.

Karalee looked away and back again. Why in the world was she so mush-minded? Then she knew. She was with the man she loved.

"I said I wasn't going to press you on the first evening," he said slowly. "But I want you to walk with me." He stood and said, "Leave the dishes," took her hand and pulled her up, then headed straight for the woods where they could have some privacy.

She noticed others were watching. "But it won't look right..." she started.

"What? That we take a walk?"

"It's just that everything is out in the open." She looked around.

122

"Well then, is there a preacher man around tonight?"

"Whatever for?" she asked.

"If he wants to marry us, we will be husband and wife. Then you won't have to worry about what others think."

Karalee felt her mouth open and then shut slowly. She had not a single word to say and noticed they were standing on the sun-speckled ground in a stand of trees beside the park.

"That's providing you say 'yes' to my proposal. Because, I *am* going to marry you Karalee Elizabeth Drayton Williams."

She looked away to gain her senses and said softly, "I'll die if you don't."

"Say that again," Jackson commanded and leaned closer.

"I said I'll die if you don't."

"That's what I thought. See, fact is, there was a preacher on the wagon I rode out with. He'd be willing."

"How do you know that?"

"Well, I asked him."

She stared at Jackson.

"I said, *'God if she's alive I'm going to marry her right here in Charleston.'* "

"I see," she said quietly. "Wouldn't it be wiser to go home? What about James and Lily, and..."

Jackson pressed two fingers over her lips. "They'll wait. I won't."

Foolishly, Karalee's thoughts flew to the dress she had on and wondered if he meant right that minute, so asked.

"I'll give you one day to put together a wedding dress if you want, but *I* don't need one. I love the woman, not the dress."

Karalee wanted to weep. Her emotions were running rampant.

"But I understand a woman's need for a dress on her wedding day," he said quickly, noting the distress on her face.

"Does Mother know?"

"Yep. We had a real nice talk while you were sleeping. I asked for your hand."

"You did?"

"Yes. I wouldn't do it any other way. She's your mother."

"And if she'd said no?"

"We would marry anyway," he said firmly. "As long as you would have me, that is."

Karalee nodded.

"As it stands...we will get married tomorrow if you can find a dress, and leave here as husband and wife. No more making decisions about your place - my place. We'll talk all that out later tonight, but we'll do everything together from now on."

Her heart hurt. Hurt from the joy she felt, from the protection he offered, and from the fact that a man loved her for who she was. God was giving her a second chance at happiness. Father and John were gone, Grandaddy and Granmama, and then Mama one day.

She couldn't help what happened next. She turned from him, pressed her hands to her face and wept.

She could feel his strong hands on her shoulders as he stood behind her and then as he slowly turned her his way and pulled her close to his chest. She could feel his heart beating. Karalee didn't care who was looking. She buried her face and released all the tension and loss. He pressed his hand to the back of her head as he gently wrapped his arms around her, slowly rocking her side to side.

Twenty-Six

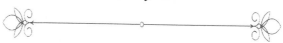

The sun was hovering just above the horizon when they returned to camp. Mother still wasn't there. Karalee watched Jackson as he went looking for the preacher. He'd left her behind to make coffee and press a fistful of water to her eyes.

Truth was, he had relished her tears, the fact he had held her close as she wept against him, wetting his shirt. Nothing would come between them ever again. When he had heard about the earthquake a full ten days after the fact, he hired a young man and his wife to finish the harvest and left James with Lily. The train took him almost to Atlanta since some of the tracks had been repaired, then he took a stage coach over the open roads, and finally arrived by wagon.

He had plenty of time to think. All the bitterness he had kept inside and all the mistakes seemed to pale against the fact he could lose the one woman still waiting for him. She did as he had asked when they were working to help free the slaves, left to settle her mother and was, he prayed, coming back to him. But he wondered, after he had at first pushed her away, if she ever would come to trust him again. Then James came. Jackson felt it was too much to ask of her: to take his child and bear the burden of his past mistakes. He had realized then she deserved someone better and determined it would not be him who would ruin her life like he had Sadie Sanderson's.

What he *hadn't* realized was that it was *he* who didn't trust her, not the other way around. *He* who had decided he wasn't good enough. *He* who determined to let her go free. When now he knew she waited and he had let her down.

As God was his witness, he would never do it again.

Taking all those thoughts into his heart, he searched for the preacher man and after finding him, asked if he might perform the ceremony...*if* Karalee agreed to it. Tomorrow at sunset, if she agreed, he repeated.

The preacher smiled and said he'd put on his best shirt, which wouldn't be much, and finish the deed. "I've got my Bible if you want to lay your hands on it," he offered.

"Bring it, Preacher," Jackson said and shook his hand. "If I find myself in hot water over how I've handled this, I'll be back and let you know."

The preacher laughed, "I'll see you tomorrow."

Jackson laughed, too, as he was waved off with a chuckle. He only hoped the man was right. Karalee deserved a more beautiful wedding, but he wanted them to be together *now*, before anything else hindered them.

When he returned to the camp, neither Mother nor Karalee was around. He asked around to learn which house was their family home. The one her Mother had longed to be near. He had walked up the street figuring they were there. When he *did* see it, he felt a pain cut into his heart. The five pillars on the front of the house were still there, but much of the house was broken and irreparable, to his way of thinking. The stairs were intact. It was nearing dark and he didn't know his way around, so headed back to the camp.

He saw Karalee's blue skirt before he saw her. She was bustling around the fire, doing something. As he moved closer he could see her stirring.

"What you are making?" he asked.

She turned slightly and looking over her shoulder said, "I'm washing."

"Ah." He leaned over and sure enough a few very womanly things were being stirred.

She pushed him away.

He took the hint, poured himself a cup of coffee from the blue tin pot that sat on a rack and found a seat on one of the tree trunks.

"Best take that one back to the man you borrowed it from," Karalee pointed. "He's got a large family."

Jackson got up, did as she bid and came back. "Where's your mother?"

"She is visiting with her friend. No doubt telling her all."

Jackson shrugged. "Let her talk. It's our wedding day tomorrow. And for all the plans she surely had for you, she must be sorely disappointed. That is, if you agree to marry me."

126

She looked up and saw his teasing smile. "I do," she said and stirred the pot.

"Well, just see that you do. I talked to the preacher and he's going to meet us down at the point just before the sun goes down. Does that suit you?"

"It suits me," she said quietly.

Jackson stood and walked over, took the stirring paddle from her hand and set it aside, turned her to him and said, "Look at me."

She did.

"You sure? Are you certain this is what you want?"

Her long pause about did him in. He began thinking of ways he could have done this differently when she said, "I said I do. And I meant it."

"You just remember those first two words tomorrow, okay?" he teased, but felt a relief in his midsection like he'd never felt before. What would he have done if she'd changed her mind?

"Have you an idea for your dress?" he asked.

"Mother and I talked a bit about it."

"Secret then?"

"Secret," she said and picked up the paddle.

"I'll leave you to your work, but mind you, I'll be down at the camp over there with the preacher and his family until tomorrow. I won't bother you. I'll find some work, stay with the men and meet you down at the point just before the sun goes down. If that's suitable for you."

"It's suitable," Karalee said.

Jackson walked away. She had said yes. And he knew she would be there. Now he had to unpack his bag and find his best shirt and pants, which wouldn't be fancy but they'd be clean.

Twenty-Seven

Jackson rose before dawn and went down to the water, found a place where he could bathe, glad for a full moon still high and bright in the sky. He smoothed his hair and pulled on a clean work shirt and trousers. He intended to work today and keep himself busy.

Before he knew it, the church tower gong sounded three times. He hadn't seen Karalee all day. But her mother was a bit short when he'd seen her and teasingly asked if he might eat dinner with them. She answered in curt words, "It is not good to see the bride on her wedding day." And off she trod. Jackson couldn't help but smile. The woman was made of tough stuff for a gentle Southern lady. He laughed and saluted her. No way was he going to give her something to carry back to Karalee.

He found a family willing to feed him in exchange for some help moving furniture.

He roamed the camp, played a game of cards with a few men sitting under the shade of a large tree, and hauled up a large thick branch to build a fire for a woman who'd lost her husband. She wanted one with a slow-burn to bake her bread on, so he created a make-shift oven with whatever scraps he could find laying around.

The day passed too slowly and he was getting nervous. He hadn't seen Karalee and hoped all was going well.

He noted when he walked by, some of the ladies were tittering behind their hands. Word must have gotten around that he was soon to be a groom. He had glanced their way, but then pretty much ignored them. It was a good sign all the ladies were talking. He knew one thing; women loved weddings and babies so everything must be going just fine.

After a fourth pass through the camp, helping wherever he could, he joined a bench full of elderly gentlemen smoking pipes and cigars at what-was-left of the General Store.

"You the one gettin' hitched?" someone asked. A puff of smoke was whipped away by the gusty wind through the open window.

"Yep."

"Got you a fine woman," another remarked.

"I know that," Jackson replied.

"See that you do," another grumped.

He heard a few words of advice, too. Among those, "It'd be best if you just walk out the door when you and your woman aren't seeing eye-to-eye."

"Aw, just give her a good kiss and she'll be fine. Works every time," one gent offered and chuckled.

Jackson was watching the sun. It was starting downward. His palms began to sweat, not from the heat of the day. Since it was Tuesday, he figured folks would be too busy to come to the ceremony. "Better get on down there," an old man nagged. "You don't want her thinkin' you're not showin' up to yer own weddin'."

Jackson stood. He didn't like the sounds of that!

He went off to change into his wedding clothes: A white shirt with a borrowed string tie, and brown trousers. A real comb was run through his hair. He had on his boots and best hat. It would have to do. At least he was clean. He headed slowly down to the point, then straight to the stand of trees, mostly for the shade. He saw ladies scurrying about. Tables had been set up—most of them from homes, some handmade from the rubble—about a dozen. He felt bad. He should have helped with those.

He smelled something really good and realized he'd hardly eaten all day, roaming from camp to camp.

Wasn't long before people started to assemble, mostly the ladies and girls, he noted. Had the word gotten that far? Then the men began to come and stand behind them. He guessed the ladies wanted to witness the whole thing, while the men were satisfied with their position at the back.

Then the preacher was walking toward him. Jackson took a look behind him. The sun was lowering. He noted the orange reflection on the clouds, trees and bushes. It was a good omen. Heart beating fast, Jackson saw the preacher motion for him to come forward. Jackson saw there was a broken pot full of field flowers on the ground up front

129

so he walked up and stood next to that. The preacher motioned for him to turn.

Jackson watched, as the crowd slowly began to part. He waited for her to appear, and suddenly she did, from way back. Her mother was at her side. They were arm in arm. Karalee had on a white dress that went all the way to the ground and white flowers in her dark hair that was wrapped all up on her head.

The dress was wide enough that folks had to stand further apart to let her through. When she was about ten feet off, Jackson saw her dark eyes and some pretty earrings that sparkled like diamonds in the sun. Her eyes were settled on him. He stood taller, straighter. She was coming to him.

As she made her way closer, he never took his eyes off hers. She had lost so much. He felt like he would never, if he could help it, let her down.

Then there she was, standing beside him, smelling heavenly. The preacher had to repeat himself twice for them to join hands. He took her soft hands into his, followed instructions, and said all the appropriate words that made them husband and wife. The wind blew her veil high up over her head at the pronouncement. He heard folks tittering, but she managed to gather it up again and hold onto it.

Then the preacher said with a smile, "You may kiss your bride if you've a mind to."

Jackson leaned down, and gently laid a kiss on his wife's sweet lips, letting the gentle fragrance of her wash over him. Then they turned toward the people.

"I present Mr. and Mrs. Jackson Woodridge."

Veil tight in her fist, he took her free hand, wrapped it in his elbow and walked straight down through the crowd as it opened to them.

After they had made their way to the end, a line formed for well-wishers who wanted to give their blessing. Then everyone dispersed.

They were standing there alone.

"I'm glad you came." He pushed strands of her windblown hair, now coming out of the pins, away from her face.

"Did you think I wouldn't?"

Her soft voice almost choked off his next words. "I would have come after you if you didn't," he said in a whisper.

130

She smiled. "I'm yours, Jackson."

He leaned in for a long, slow kiss and was interrupted by voices. People were coming back with food. Before long the entire group was eating quickly, before the sun disappeared below the horizon.

Then just as if the whole thing had been planned months ahead of time, folks carried off their tables and took home their dishes.

Even Mama had left.

"So what now?" Karalee asked.

Jackson looked at her. "I never made a plan," he realized.

We'll go back to Mother's," Karalee said quietly. "We have the rest of our lives...." her voice trailed off.

Arm in arm, they walked back, barely able to see. The camp was noisy again with people talking, some cleaning up by firelight, others snoring in their tents, but all a little happier, it seemed to Karalee.

"Mother's not here," she said as she opened the flap to their abode.

"She's staying with her friends," Jackson said. "One of the ladies carried her message to me."

"She didn't mind?"

"She wrote she couldn't stand it if I snored, so she'd stay down there a couple days."

Karalee felt her face flush.

The whole camp was around them. There was no way they could consummate their marriage.

Jackson must have read her mind, "Don't worry. I'll sleep on the floor inside and you can have the sofa. It's a whole lot softer, plus I made a new cover over it in case the dew comes."

"I saw you'd made another canopy-type thing," she said.

"First I want us to sit outside on that sofa so we can talk. Then when everyone else has shut down for the night, we'll kiss goodnight. Better go in there and change."

Karalee took her wedding dress off and hung it over a chair inside the tent, changed into her pink flowered dress and came out.

Jackson drew her to the sofa and they sat.

They were quiet for a while, listening to babies cry, dogs barking, and low voices as the camp quieted. "Where did you get that dress?"

"It was my mother's on her wedding day. We brought it in her trunk. It was a bit dusty, but we shook it and aired it out overnight."

131

"It's beautiful."

"I tried to imagine Father seeing Mother coming down the aisle in it."

Jackson saw her eyes fill. "You were thinking of him and John weren't you?"

"How did you know?"

"Lily told me about your Father. I could see when you spoke of him that you were close. And you mentioned once or twice how he taught you to handle the accounts."

"You remember that?"

"I do."

They talked on into the night and then Karalee said, "It's time to get some sleep."

Jackson stood and pulled her up straight into his arms. Kissed her like a married man, and set her away from him.

In a few minutes, she was safely on the sofa, with light covers and a last kiss.

As he walked away from her, he looked skyward and whispered, "God, I know you're up there. I don't know you very well, but I thank you for her." He ducked into the tent and lay down on the pallet she had made for him. Karalee was his wife.

Twenty-Eight

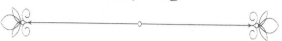

Jackson rose early and saw Karalee was still sleeping, so he went to work helping some of the men remove a wall that was dangerously close to falling into the street where children played nearby.

When it was finished, the group of men decided they would walk on down the way and check other buildings that needed immediate attention. The wagons were still hauling away bricks, piling up broken ones in one area to use for fill and the unbroken ones to be used for rebuilding.

After several hours, he came back to the camp and found Karalee cooking with several other ladies. The cauldron at her place was full to the brim with something that smelled very much like fish soup, which he hated.

That meant, he learned from some of the men, that vittles were getting low. It was difficult to feed hundreds of people. Some of the folks with lesser damaged homes had moved in and allowed others to be inside; especially those with nursing infants and small children. In other cases, homes had to be completely rebuilt. It would take years to recover.

Thinking thus, he headed toward Karalee and coming up behind her, slipped his hands around her waist. She startled at first and then shimmied out of his arms...other ladies were watching. He smiled, took off his hat, slapped it against his leg and then resettled it.

"You hungry?" she asked, holding her hand up to block the sun.

"You bet. Smells like fish soup."

"It is," she said firmly. "It's all we have. The wagonload of cabbages and potatoes is gone. I think a lot of the ladies fixed special meals for our wedding," she whispered to him. "Now they don't have much."

Jackson let her know with his eyes that he understood the problem. "I can borrow a wagon and head back to Atlanta, see if anybody else can go along. It'll take me a few days."

"Would you Jackson? I'm sure it would help. The gardens are at peak, but we've cleaned them out, so if anyone has extra, I know it would lift spirits around here. Some of the folks are down to cornmeal and water."

"I'll see what I can do." He turned to leave.

"Jackson, if you have time could you drive out to Philomena's and see how she, Hayward and Judith are doing?" She gave him directions.

He nodded, gave her a look, and left the women to their fish soup.

Several hours later he had commitments from sixteen men and six wagons. They were just lining up to head down the road. Seems everyone was running out of food and supplies. Folks were getting sick, too. Dysentery. Karalee worried that it may be the water, though they had been boiling it. Some of the folks were eating near-rotten fish just to survive. She'd heard that from the ones who were the poorest.

Lifting her apron, Karalee wiped sweat from her brow. She wasn't feeling the best after eating that soup. Jackson came and let her know they were about to leave.

"Philomena and the kids are doing fine. They've got enough food," he reported.

"Good. I was concerned since I didn't see them at the wedding."

"They probably didn't get word," Jackson said.

"You're right. Please be careful."

"You look a little peaked. You all right?"

"Just a little light-headed. I don't think that fish soup is settling well in my stomach."

"Well, see to it you rest some in the shade, and then get in the tent and have a nap. Can't afford to have my wife sick when we travel home."

Karalee looked at him and almost burst into tears. She didn't want to leave everyone here. They needed help. And Mother would be alone, Grandaddy and Granmama only days in their graves.

Jackson saw the trouble, pulled her off to a stand of trees, pressed her against a huge Live Oak and waited for her to think. She wasn't well, he could see that.

"You know we have to get back to Michigan soon."

She nodded but didn't look at him, instead looked over his shoulder.

"We haven't had a chance to talk."

Karalee pulled her gaze to his eyes.

"I've got help but only for a month. The entire year's harvest will be lost if I don't get back."

"I know," she said quietly. "I know...it's just hard. Mother will have no family here. Her brothers, Grandaddy and Granmama are gone and now I am leaving." She pressed her forehead to his chest.

"I can't leave you here, Karalee. Not now. All the way here I worried I might not find you alive. And when I did...I knew one thing; we would be married. I want you where I am."

Karalee looked up into his eyes. He was hurting, too.

"I feel the same, Jackson. I wondered if I'd ever see you again."

"Then we know it was the right thing to do?" he asked gently. "Yes."

"Then let's do all we can while we're here...but in a week we need to be heading back. I'll try to get more help. You can have a talk with your Mother when she comes back tomorrow night."

"Okay." Karalee squared her shoulders, slowly pulled away from the tree and started back to camp.

"What are you going to do?" Jackson followed alongside her.

"Mrs. George needs help with her children. They are gravely ill."

"You're not to go." Jackson stopped and with his hands on her upper arms turned her. "You don't look well yourself. And it's bad enough with dysentery. It'll spread like wildfire through the camp. Go lie down, save your strength."

"But..."

"Lie down." Jackson said firmly and walked her into the tent. "I'm throwing this blanket over the top so the sun doesn't beat down through that thin sheet overhead. I want you to get some rest. You won't be good to anyone if you fall apart."

Karalee was too tired to argue. She started to loosen the strings of her dress and Jackson took hold of her, turned her around and unlaced

135

the strings at her back, sat her down, took off her shoes and settled her before he would leave.

"I'll be back in a few days. I expect to see you rested and feeling better."

"Yes," she said, eyelids too heavy to keep open, especially when Jackson threw that large dark blanket across the top of the tent. It was like she was in her own bedroom back home.

Jackson waited until she was asleep, packed a couple items of clothing, made sure his pistol was loaded and stuffed in a side pocket, and then went out to meet the men who had brought their rifles. He talked to the guys and asked what chance they had of getting a wild pig.

Several men knew where to look and there were plenty of woods around. Most of them were still in town clearing up debris and burying the dead, which finally slowed to a trickle, they hadn't even thought to go out and get meat.

Jackson hated to waste the time, but felt it might brighten spirits. The people were getting tired of living in tents, working dawn to dusk. There had been a great deal of progress, yet it was wearing them down.

It took an hour to get to pig country, but John James Hopkins knew exactly where to look, and it seemed as though the earthquake had also affected the animals. They were foraging for food themselves since most of the outlying fields were damaged.

They hauled in two wild pigs and once word got around, the people gathered to help. Jackson smiled and headed to the tent.

"Ah, you return," he said, and dipped his hat to Karalee's Mother.

"As I said I would," she shot back. "Karalee's not feeling well. I tried to talk her into coming into the house for a while, but she said the dust is too much and preferred to sleep in the tent."

"She'll be fine in there," Jackson said firmly and stepped inside to let her know he was late, but they were headed out. She was still asleep. He pulled a strand of hair off her damp cheek and hoped she would be all right.

"The men are waiting. I'll be back in a few days," he informed her mother. The meat will need processing."

"Where are you going?"

He noted her stance, hands on hips. "Atlanta. We're going to bring back some food and medicines. We're going to need both."

"See to it." She shooed him off and about the time he turned his back she said, "You didn't touch her did you?"

Jackson stopped in his tracks, turned and looked her in the eye. "Ma'am, that would be none of your business." Best to set her straight right from the start.

Jackson dipped his hat to her again. That was one tough woman. She was just ornery enough to make it out here in this mess, even if she was a high society woman. He gave her that at least.

He met the men and another wagon joined up. They needed more tools and more clothes. Some of the folks had lost everything when a fire from one of the downed lines burned an entire street of businesses, houses and barns.

The trip was successful. By the time they gathered tools, seeds to plant for spring, clothing, soap, fresh food, rice, flour, beans, a couple of dairy cows, and more chickens, there might be enough to keep them going. There would be plenty of eggs and chicken to eat. The trip took nearly eight days, one day of rain making travel slow on the way back.

The good news was several young single men from the Quaker community loaded up four wagons of vegetables from their gardens, sacks of flour in abundance, even some flower seeds for the ladies to plant, and quilts the woman had pulled off their own beds. One wagon was full to overflowing with potatoes and cabbages.

When all the wagons pulled in the people rushed over: there was a lot of hand shaking. The wagons formed a line right down the center of town to let folks help themselves.

Jackson looked up and saw Karalee. She was smiling. It did him good to hold her and feel her soft cheek against his. He pushed her back to have a look. "You look much better, smell good, too."

"I finally had time to go down and get a bath."

Jackson was going to have a hard time keeping his hands to himself, her all soft and sweet smelling like she was.

Twenty-Nine

It took an entire day to distribute the goods, things given to the poor first, and clothes were given to those most in need. Jackson noted that was where character showed up. Some who had plenty took what they didn't need. Others less fortunate were kind enough to share what little they had. Trouble brought out the best and worst in a person. It was the way of human nature, he finally decided.

They had roasted one pig and set jars tightened under cold water to keep the leftover meat. It wouldn't last long, so they opened a bag of beans and set the ham to boiling adding onions and carrots.

Jackson went with the men to set tables up and down the streets. They stretched out in two long rows, on either side of the wagons. The women said it made cooking and carrying easier. There would be a celebration in the town tonight.

At the end of the day, the people gathered bedding for the young men who had come to help.

It was time to find Karalee. She had been put in charge of the community pot to make sure the beans didn't burn while cooking all day.

He went back to her and said, "Wouldn't be surprised if we had visitors tonight, the four legged kind...smelling all the food."

"I don't doubt it. Next thing you know, we'll be having alligator soup." She smiled.

"Good to see you feeling better."

"Yes, I think the fish was bad, Jackson. Good thing you didn't eat it. Several of us suffered afterward."

"You remember what I said about leaving?" He brought up the subject.

"Yes, I remember. Mother and I talked. I declare, Jackson, she's as she was at home. Didn't want to talk about it. Said I had to do what I had to do, like I was abandoning her."

He listened.

"I guess I feel as though I am."

"She's a grown woman."

"Yes, I know. But she's my mother."

"And *you're* a grown woman," he said quietly, giving her time to think about that.

"I...am. I always felt like I was the mother and she was the child," Karalee said, as though just realizing it.

"Seemed that way to me," he stated, and added more wood to the fire beneath the pot. "Think those beans are done?"

"Why, you hungry?" She knew that would set him off.

"After days on the road? You bet I am! That smell's been gnawing at me all afternoon."

She dished him up a bowl. "Can't have a man going hungry." She smiled.

Jackson's heart felt a lurch. He still couldn't believe he was married. Said he never would wed. A fear snatched at his conscience. What if he turned out to be the kind of husband his father was. He shoved that thought right out of his head. He was *not* his father.

His wife handed him the soup. As he looked up, he silently prayed he would be a good husband for her. "Thanks."

"Eat and enjoy. There's plenty, she said quietly.

Jackson felt an overwhelming sense of joy pass through his heart. She had married *him*. That must mean something. Even if she had turned him down twice.

"Have you heard from Lily?

"No, I told her not to write unless the news was bad. Mail service is just beginning to get straightened out. As long as they're okay, I'm good. James knows it may be awhile. But he's so new away from the man he thought was his father, I don't want to leave him any longer than I have to."

Karalee, sitting on a tree trunk, pressed her hands together in her lap. "I don't want that either."

"We'll manage," he said and handed her the empty bowl. "Now have some yourself."

She had one spoonful, but wasn't that hungry after smelling it all afternoon.

"Where's your Mother?"

139

She's down at Mrs. Bonhoeffers. They'll be going together to the celebration. It seems they have much in common."

"Such as?" Jackson asked and downed a cupful of water.

"Such as children who don't meet their standards," she said quietly.

Somehow the words hit home. He could never please his own father. How his mama had tried to bring the two of them together...a man and his son. And all she'd gotten was belittling talk and pushed around for her intervention.

His father was an angry man. Had been for as long as Jackson could remember.

He realized he had been musing. "Let them commiserate. It's good for them to think they're right. Just don't take it on, okay? You're the woman I love. I don't want you worrying about what your mother thinks of you. She'll never agree with you, no matter what you do."

He looked around to see her face; she was considering what he'd just said.

"I think you're right," she said softly. "She and I will never be alike, however we try. Perhaps I should just stop trying."

"You love your mother. I see it in all you do. But you aren't her. You're two different people," he said wisely, and then realized he needed to listen to his own words. He and his father were two different people, too. That gave him a little comfort. He was *not* his father. Lily told him that all the time. He just hadn't believed it was true until now.

* * *

The people welcomed two more wagons from Quakers who heard about the needs of Charleston's people. They arrived at dusk. The town was awake long into the night. Karalee slept in the tent with Mother. Jackson took the sofa.

The next morning, Karalee rose early and walked to Mother's house, gathered some things she wanted to take home and brought them back to the tent: a daguerreotype of her grandparents, with Mother's permission of course, a few clothes and one of grandmother's teapots, hoping it would make it back home in one piece.

She showed Jackson and he wrapped the teapot up in an old shirt and put it in his bag. Watching him do it, Karalee felt her heart warm. He reminded her so much of her father. Gentle. Wise. No-nonsense when necessary. Her heart swelled.

Back to work, the days flew by.

"Karalee, we leave in two days," Jackson reminded her. "I've been letting people know we are headed out. Several want to go with us as far as Atlanta. One newly married couple wants to take his bride to his parents' house. They were going to settle here, but..." He shrugged. "The other couple has three children. They were visiting her parents here when the quake struck. They want to go home."

Karalee nodded. "I'll talk to Mother again tonight."

"Do what you can, but if she gives you any trouble, I will talk to her," Jackson said and added, "I'm heading out to see what I can do. I'll be back by dinnertime."

Karalee watched him walk down the street, and then stop at the church on the corner. Some men were trying to pull down a tree that had uprooted and was leaning too near the church. He hurried to get behind and pull on the rope. The church would be destroyed if that tree fell the wrong way.

She bit her tongue, watching as other men saw the problem and ran. Finally the gnarly tree fell within a foot of the building. After a collective sigh and a few handshakes, the men began to hand saw the branches. Of all the things she'd experienced in her life, Karalee felt this was one of the best. So much loss. So many deaths. Yet for those who still toiled on the earth, there was a singular joy: people who cared for each other. She felt changed. She had never lived outdoors a day in her life and now she had survived almost six weeks outside. She was doing things she'd never done before. Father would have been proud of her and Mother. Which reminded her, she needed to talk to her.

After a few inquiries, she learned Mother was visiting an elderly couple she must have known, for when Karalee walked up she could tell by the conversation they were old friends.

She was introduced and then she knew exactly who they were: the parents of the young man Mama had loved. Before she met Father.

In a moment of weakness or kindness, Karalee didn't know which, Mother told her she had wanted to marry this young man, but her parents forbade it, preferring she marry Father instead.

Karalee learned later Mother's parents were sure they could convince the handsome graduate of the Citadel to reside with their daughter here in Charleston. Grandaddy offered him a job, in fact, which he turned down, preferring to return to his home state of Michigan. Devastated, they had been disappointed to the degree they almost disenfranchised their own daughter, thinking he must have married to gain their money. When time proved differently, which took years, the damage had already been done. Mother hated Michigan and the fact she had not been allowed to marry the man she wanted.

Karalee kept that in mind when she left them to their visit, and reminded Mother she would be waiting after dinner for their talk.

Mother had waved her off, too busy to be interrupted.

Thirty

At dinner Jackson came walking up, dusty and smiling.

"What are you smiling about?" Mother asked, grumping at him.

"Nothing important," he told her as he rinsed his hands in a bowl of water, splashed some in his face and toweled dry.

Karalee set a plate in front of him and dished out chicken and a potato baked from the fire. "Whoa, fit for a king!" he exclaimed, to which Mother shook her head.

He ate and announced he was going to play a few games of chess with some of the men and let the girls talk.

Karalee sensed this was not going to go well, but ignored her fears and said, "Mother, it's time. We must make a plan."

"I will make my own plans, Karalee," she said sharply. "How do you think I have made it thus far?"

"I know, Mother. You are a strong woman. But you forget, you taught me how to be strong, too."

"Too much so," she shot back.

"Be that as it may, Jackson and I are heading back to Michigan. He has a harvest to bring in. And his son is waiting."

Mother sipped her tea and acted as though she had not spoken.

"Will you be all right here? You will need money to repair the house. Thankfully, your home was spared for the most part. At least the roof is intact and the pillars still in place."

"I have money. Do you think our family destitute? I surmise it is why you have never realized what a family line you derive from."

"Mother I know you have royalty in your family. But what good does that do when one has nothing?"

"I also have the summer cottage in Newport, which I plan to sell. That sale and the plantation sale will more than bring back Grandaddy's and Granmama's house to its original grandeur."

Karalee disliked all the fancy words. One could have grandeur and splendor all around and still not be happy, satisfied, or even at peace. That fact became clearer every day.

"I know you want to stay here. But I am going to say this anyway. You are welcome to come home anytime," Karalee offered.

Mother looked at her harshly. "I *am* home," she spit out. "Michigan was never my home."

Karalee nodded and felt tears prick her eyes, but she would not let Mother get to her. They had had such warm moments after the quake, places where their hearts seemed to touch, even if just for a few hours.

Her severity, Karalee assumed, must be protection of her right to stay or go. And it was true. Mother had her choices. But so did she.

"You're right, Mother. Home is where your heart wants to stay. And I knew you were never happy there. It is just the way of it. I will leave, knowing you are happiest here." She smiled, suddenly calm. "And I will go because my home is with Jackson."

Mother stood, wrapped her shawl around her narrow shoulders — her dark hair shining in the sun and beautiful eyes so blue and determined. Karalee watched as she limped away.

The way of the world was this: one had to do what one was meant to do. She stood. The talk was over. She and Jackson would pull out before sun-up two days hence.

That evening, Mother had trotted off to Mrs. Bonhoeffers, she was sure, to tell her the news. Jackson came back some time later and they sat on the sofa together, coffee in his cup and tea in hers, while Karalee told him all.

He listened and after a time of quiet, said, "All will be well. You are safe with me."

"I know," she said softly as the sun crept below the horizon and disappeared in the space of a minute.

He pitched the last bit of coffee from his cup, put it on top of a barrel and took her hand. "Let's go for a walk." He pulled her close and tucked her hand in his elbow.

Karalee didn't say a word. Just listened to the night sounds. Frogs chirping near the green waters. The trees were barely moving, the land and air still hot and heavy from the day's sun. The dogs weren't even barking. The camp had settled down early.

144

"I do love the peacefulness," she said after a while.

Jackson thought and after a time asked, "Will you be happy in Michigan?"

"Of course," she answered quickly and squeezed his arm, feeling his strength. "I'll have you...and James." She smiled in the dark. "I wonder how he's doing."

"Yeah, he's a pretty good kid."

"Like his father," Karalee said quietly, and felt a new sense of amazement. Jackson had a son and she was Mrs. Jackson Clay Woodridge. She hadn't even written her new name yet, let alone considered herself someone's mother.

"Do you think your mother will be all right?" Jackson asked as he turned them around and headed back.

"Yes, I do. Nothing has broken her yet. Marrying the wrong man, going after Rutledge, getting shot herself." Karalee shook her head. "She will be all right. She's a survivor."

"So is her daughter," Jackson said.

Karalee stopped. "Explain that, please," she said firmly.

"Think about it. You survived *her*. You survived the pressure to force you into a marriage. The fact she would have disowned you if she would have known what you were doing with the slaves. You lost your father whom you loved and your brother. I'd say you can call yourself a survivor."

When she was quiet for a long time, Jackson felt uneasy. Had he said something hurtful?

"I guess when you put it like that. . ." she said quietly. "I just hadn't quite thought of it that way."

"It's easy to see how things are with other people. But hard to see ourselves."

"You're right."

When Jackson heard her quiet laugh in the dark, he stopped her, turned her around and with hands on either side of her face, kissed her like he always wanted to...away from prying eyes, like a man kissed his wife. He heard her soft sigh when they started walking again. It was enough for him.

Soon enough they would be away.

The day before their leaving, people came by the tent and said their goodbyes and handed them bread wrapped in a towel, a gunnysack of potatoes, several cabbages, a gift here and there, words of wisdom, and finally wishes and prayers for safe travel.

Jackson had brought Philomena, Hayward and Judith down in a small wagon for dinner. They had eaten together, then at dark their guests headed back to Summerville.

Karalee wished she could take all three back with them. But alas, their hearts were here, too.

She and Mother said their goodbyes earlier in the day and Mother had gone home to work on her house. Karalee felt that it was more about her mother wanting to let them know she didn't need them and would be fine. When she'd tried to lay her hand on Mother's arm, she pulled it away and went to work.

It was Karalee's last wish they could at least share a parting that left both parties in good graces.

Later in the day Karalee wandered over to the house and started sweeping up dust. Most of the glass had long been cleared away, with the help of the folks in the neighborhood. The contents had been destroyed, but the structure of Mother's house had survived with light damage to the outside, which was fixable when people got back to their lives. Karalee picked up the dust and tossed it out in the backyard. She looked around pressing to memory the way the house looked now. Mother was upstairs. She went up and found her throwing out old papers and books.

"Mother, are you sure you want to toss Grandaddy's books?"

She was silent and then looked up. "What is that to you? This is never where you wanted to be."

She watched as Mother tossed another book and another into an old crate.

"Would you mind if I chose some to keep as a remembrance of Grandaddy and Granmama?"

"What for? They meant nothing to you. You never cared that they hoped to see you love this place as much as they did."

"Mother, I *did* love this place. When I visited as a child, I loved being with Grandaddy and Granmama, too." Karalee cringed at the fact Mother couldn't see it.

Her mother's disapproval fell heavy on her soul. She thought about it for a minute and said, "Mother this house was meant for *you. They* meant it for you. They wanted their little girl back. That's all

146

they had left. They must have been so sad when Samuel died and Henderson never returned."

"Hence my desire to come home," she said.

Karalee saw the firm set of her mother's chin. The look of determination. "This house was *always* yours."

"Well, it's about time you see it my way," she said, looking down her nose.

"I do, Mama. I see it your way."

With that, her mother walked down the stairs and out to the gardens. Karalee followed.

"Here is a start from my Dogwood. See that you keep it moist. Plant that tree and every time you look at it, know I am happy here in my house."

Karalee took the branch and waited while mother wet an old shirt and wrapped it. "Thank you." She paused, started to turn and turned back. She looked into her eyes and knew this was the moment. "Mama, I would like to hug you. We leave before light tomorrow."

"Well, get on with it then," she said.

Karalee reached up and put her arms around her mother's neck, kissed the side of her face and let go. She was stone-stiff. But at least she had done it. "I know you did what you could and I'm grateful." She thought she saw her mother's eyes blink a couple of times and hoped that their parting would never be regretful.

Karalee turned and walked away. She looked back, but Mother was already chopping dead branches off the Dogwood. "Bless Mother and her house, Lord."

Thirty-One

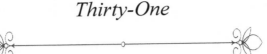

When Karalee returned to camp, she found Jackson pulling down the tent they had stayed in for several weeks. Families were slowly returning to their homes.

"Your mother told me to disassemble the camp. She is going to stay in her house. Have you said your goodbyes?"

"We have."

"I see it did not go very well." He stopped working for a moment.

"It went as expected," she said, and showed him the branch.

"What is that for?"

"It's from her Dogwood tree. She wants me to plant it in Michigan."

"It'll probably survive," he said, and heard his wife say...

"It might at that."

"Keep it moist. Once we get to Atlanta we will be able to go back by train," he reminded her.

"That sounds lovely." She got to work. There was much to do yet.

They finished late in the evening.

"Shall we just go?" he suggested. "We've no place to sleep and I don't want to impose on anyone at this late hour. We would make a few miles in the coolness, and there is a sliver of moon to light the way."

"I would love that, Jackson." Karalee smiled. "We have done what we could, have we not?"

"I believe we have," he said, and hooked up the team.

The camp had dwindled down in the last couple of days as folks, anxious to be home, moved back into houses that still needed repair. But at least there would be no more quakes and families could start over.

Jackson clucked to the horses, signaling them to head out, turned the wagon around and as quietly as possible, started on down the road. Karalee let her head fall onto Jackson's shoulder, but soon found that it was too much work to keep it there. They were traveling over hard dirt and ruts formed by the many wagons coming from Atlanta. He laughed, handed her the reins, folded a shirt around his hand, and then stuck it on top of his shoulder for her head. After a time, she was stiff and crawled in the back, found a blanket and a small spot to lie down.

By daylight, she was sore and hardly able to move, but the wagon had stopped. They were near a town. She could hear voices and lifted her head to peek out.

Her husband was talking to someone. He motioned for her to join him, and came to help her off the back of the wagon. "There's a place to eat. Mrs. Wiley serves boarders and said we could come there for breakfast."

Karalee straightened her hair, smoothed her skirt and yawned, glad they were alone at the moment. Didn't seem like much going on in the little town.

Mrs. Wiley was a tall woman. Her laugh was hearty and she was talkative. Jackson even laughed out loud at some of her comments. Seems Mrs. Wiley was just glad those Yankees had left town. She'd had to feed them once. Said they were just boys...fed 'em rightly and prayed they went home. "Sorry if I offend anyone," she said, and practically yelled out, "If no one wants any more pancakes, this is the last of 'em I'm cookin'."

They used her outhouse before they left and were back on the road again, full. And with a shortcut, were sure to make their trip half a day shorter a man claimed. Jackson decided it was worth it and headed out.

Five days later they arrived in Atlanta. It was the middle of the night. Karalee had taken her place on the pallet she used for a bed.

Jackson decided to travel further until daylight, at which time he pulled up to a hotel, the sun just up. There were already people inside eating. So he woke Karalee and advised her they were at their destination.

"We're in Atlanta?" she asked and sat up.

"One and the same," Jackson said, passing his rough hand over his face. "I need a bath."

"That sounds so good." Karalee stepped off the wagon and on weak legs, walked across a real boardwalk and into a real hotel with a small restaurant. It felt strange and she said so.

"The train station is just down the road," he informed her as they walked inside, found a small table and sat down. "I'll turn in the wagon and the horses, and then we'll be on our own with what we can carry. I'll pay the man to return the wagon."

Karalee ate like a starved woman and relished the fact they would actually be on a train. She'd almost forgotten what comfort was like. The idea of being clean, dressed in decent clothes and rolling across the miles on a train was almost more than she could bear.

"We're staying the night," Jackson informed her. "I arranged to have a bath brought up."

"All night? A bath?" She sipped tea from a china cup and moaned in relief.

"Yep. One night. We need rest."

She finished her food and found her eyelids were heavy.

Jackson stood, told her to wait at the table and walked to the counter, paid the man and came back swinging a key.

"Our room is ready," he said and pulled back her chair as she stood.

The climb up the stairs was slow, each step a practice in motivation. After eating all that food, she could hardly maneuver. Jackson either.

He keyed open the door and in front of them stood a made-up bed with a clean quilt, rugs on the wood floor, windows with curtains, and a tin tub in the middle of the room, steam rising up from it.

Karalee feasted her eyes.

"You go first," Jackson said.

"You don't mind?"

"No, I'll go down and get our tickets. I don't want to miss that train," he said and walked out.

"Karalee set her valise down and inside of ten minutes was in the bath. She was half asleep when she heard the key at the door, rose up as fast as her legs would allow and grabbed her towel, then dashed behind the screen where she'd placed her clothes.

"Can I come in?"

"No," she said while drying herself off with a towel.

He chuckled and reminded her they were married.

She huffed at that, and then heard him enter.

A minute later… "Okay, I'm getting in."

She ignored him, slipped her gown on and took her time combing out her hair, then realized: they were alone for the first time.

She and Mother had never talked about anything personal. It took him forever…she was tired of sitting behind the screen, so spoke up. He snorted and stood, water sluicing off him. Soon he said she could come out if she wished.

"Of course, I wish," she grumbled. "I'm tired and want to lie down."

She peeked around the screen to make sure he was decent and stepped out, her wrapper over her gown held closed in a tight fist.

His hair was wet and combed back. He looked so handsome as he stood there gazing out the window. He had put on trousers and a shirt. And he hadn't yet turned. She hurried behind him and headed for the bed, slid under the covers and said, "You may turn around now."

Jackson forced himself to wipe the smirk off his face. He doubted very much her Mother had talked of such things with her and smiled.

She, on the other hand, decided to turn her back and sleep. Except…she couldn't. He sat in a chair and read a town newspaper, every now and again telling her about something he read.

When the room began to darken, Karalee felt the bed move. She froze. But he climbed in slowly, turned, and was snoring within a few minutes. Finally, she could sleep.

* * *

It seemed she had been asleep in that wonderfully soft, sweet-smelling bed for five minutes when she heard someone calling her name.

"Wake up, Karalee. I woke late. We have to catch that train."

She tried to bring her mind to the surface but didn't wish to. Who was calling her anyway?

Train?

151

"Oh my goodness, why didn't you wake me?" she shot out of bed and almost landed on her face, her feet entangled in the bedding.

"Don't break anything," he said as he pulled on his trousers, shirt and suspenders.

She threw the wrapper around herself, snatched the dress she had, thankfully, laid out last evening, and headed for the screen. Inside of twenty minutes they were downstairs grabbing a few biscuits and running for the train.

Once they were safely boarded, they relaxed. "We made it," she said and asked for another biscuit.

Thirty-Two

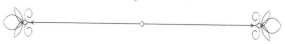

By the time the train pulled into Chicago, Karalee was downright crabby. And they still had to wait for the train to Niles. Jackson had been so patient. There was a three-hour delay now. He suggested they eat, but she wanted nothing more than to lie down somewhere. Jackson insisted, so she followed him to the small dining area and to a table.

When the food was put down, she ate like a starving woman while maintaining her manners in public, but hungry nonetheless.

"Glad we sat down, I see," Jackson teased her.

She looked away, put her fork down, and tapped her napkin to her lips. "As you see," she said smartly.

"A woman scorned, a woman hungry..." He left that hanging in the air.

She gave him a look that said if they were not in public...

He paid the worker, took her elbow and led her back down to the waiting area. "Lay your head on my shoulder," he said quietly. Karalee wanted to refuse on principle alone, but couldn't seem to find the wherewithal to do so, and did as he asked.

Sometime later she lifted her head and saw some people looking at her. She straightened her hair, looked down, made sure she was buttoned up and looked to Jackson.

"You were snoring," he said.

"I was not."

"You were," he said calmly.

She straightened and made sure not to look at the patrons. *Snoring indeed!* Then horrified, she wiped a bit of spittle from the corner of her mouth. So it was true. She pulled out a newspaper from the last stop and hid her face.

"Paper's upside down," Jackson said out of the corner of his mouth.

153

She folded it, turned it over and put it up again.

And she was angry at him. For what reason, she had no idea. She had never been this tired before.

Finally, they boarded the last train, hours late. They were almost home. Because of the late arrival, the Niles station was closed and there were no wagons or horses to be had. What now?

"We'll wait until morning. It's a short walk to the Pike Hotel on Fourth and Main. Comes recommended and best thing is, we can walk there."

Karalee walked beside him. It was indeed a short walk and much colder here than Charleston, she noted, pulling Jackson's coat closed at her neck.

"I remember when you first discovered my work," Jackson said.

"I do, too. The first time we met," she said. "You were *not* happy."

"I was not," he agreed.

The brisk walk gave her a second wind.

"The hotel lights are on. We'll be home tomorrow," Jackson assured her.

Karalee picked up her pace. "A cup of tea, even at this late hour would be wonderful."

Jackson pressed the ringer on the counter and someone came immediately. Within ten minutes, a boy had come for their bags and carried them to the elevator. The door was keyed and they were in a room. Karalee threw her valise on the floor and gave Jackson his coat back. "I don't care about tea. I just want to sleep," she said and began unbuttoning her dress. Jackson turned his back and waited for her, rather surprised at her boldness. "Do not turn," she warned and climbed into bed in her underthings. He then began to undress and she turned her back, certain she would be asleep by the time he climbed in.

And indeed she must have been, for she remembered nothing until morning. There were voices in the hallways, hushed, yes, but people were already getting around.

Breakfast. She turned and Jackson was not next to her. He must have gone down. Quickly, she got up, put on the same dress and was re-braiding her hair when he came through the door.

"There's a nice breakfast room downstairs."

154

"I'll be finished in a minute," she said.

Then they went down together and ate.

"I've arranged for a carriage. There is a service here in town."

She looked at her husband, in fact had to remember that he was, indeed, her husband, and nearer to home, felt shy. There would be no more delays. Karalee looked away for a moment and when she saw his tender gaze upon her, excitement welled up.

"It is a very nice hotel," she mentioned.

"Very nice, indeed."

"When does the carriage come?"

"One will be available in two hours or so."

"What shall we do until then?

"We'll walk along the Saint Joseph River," he said and caught her hand, led her out and down the main street. "Some of my meetings took place here. When someone from the Niles area needed a canoe ride downriver, I'd take them."

She nodded. He was sharing more of his life with her. Intrigued, she asked a few questions. Now that the war was over, people could look to the future.

"What were your thoughts about me then...in the early days?" Jackson asked.

Standing on the Main Street Bridge over the river, Karalee mused for a few moments before speaking. "I thought you sullen and unkind at first. Then, as I saw what you were doing, I began to admire you for it."

He nodded but did not look her way. Mesmerized by the flowing water or tiredness or perhaps both, they walked back up the hill and waited for the carriage on the corner of Main and Fourth Street.

It arrived and one young man brought their bags out from the hotel on cue and tied them safely to the back of the wagon.

Karalee was too excited to sleep now, her eyes gazing out the small window, recognizing the familiar area. She could have shouted for joy. Finally, there in front of her was Mama's house.

She had left the skeleton key underneath the potted plant on the front verandah and showed Jackson. He retrieved it, saying that it was a foolish place to leave it. Everyone knew keys were under potted plants.

A smile crept to her lips. Tired as she was, it was a strange thing to know he was going to follow her inside and stay.

Before she could think another thought, she found herself lifted up in his arms, her skirts flying. He gave her a look, his face inches from hers, kissed her soundly and managed to get them both through the front door before he put her down, after which, he kissed her again.

"I've brought you home Mrs. Woodridge."

Thirty-Three

When he finally *did* put her down, Karalee was quite dizzy. She steadied herself with a hand on the wall and looked around. Jackson said he was going out to the smokehouse and bringing in some beefsteak for dinner. She heard the door slam. Oh, the comforts of one's own home.

All the years began to pass before her. Papa at the table, Mama complaining that he didn't take his boots off at the door, John running through with his bow and arrow chasing a mouse that somehow got into the house. The Christmas tree in the same corner every year. The gifts that had been under them through the years.

Suddenly, she felt the weight of what lay ahead of her. This house, their family growing up here.

But it would always be *Mama's House*. Karalee regained her balance and walked around the room. Memories flooded from every corner. And Mama wasn't here. Had she done the right thing leaving her behind?

Would Jackson want to live here? She shuddered. Of course not. He had his own land and his farms. He would not know what to do with himself in town. She hadn't thought of it until just now. Would she have to sell Mama's House? She couldn't think of it right now.

The sounds of Jackson's footsteps as he came through the kitchen touched her so deeply, she wondered that she had not seen the man he was before this. She had come to the conclusion he had changed his mind about her, when now she knew, he had loved her from the beginning.

When he appeared, she ran her eyes over his face. He looked so happy, she wanted to toss convention to the air and, well, that would have to wait. He had the look of a hungry man.

She pulled off her hat and set it aside. "I'm going to change and then I'll cook."

"I'll get the bags off the front steps and bring them in."

Karalee ran upstairs. Suddenly her girlhood room flashed before her. She thought of her journal hidden beneath the floor. It would be hidden no more. Quickly, she changed into a soft pink dress, the one Jackson liked, and headed to the kitchen. The pump would have to be restarted.

He had brought wood in sometime while she was musing, she noticed because it sat on top of the oven, waiting for it to be lit. A knock at the door brought Laura.

"We are so glad to see you home. Here's a cake. I just finished it. I must go study and we don't want to interrupt your homecoming," she said and was gone.

Karalee raised her hand to stop her, to tell her Jackson was here and that they were married, but she had dashed away. She stowed her hat and wrap in the closet.

Jackson came in the back door and lit the oven as she unwrapped the meat, put two large potatoes aside, and reveled in the fact she was home. Her husband gathered wood from the back and lit up two fireplaces with a few pieces to send the chill out. The house began to warm slowly.

They sat down together at the huge dining table and ate heartily. "I was famished," she said leaning back against the chair.

"And I," Jackson said quietly.

She stood and picked up the dishes and he watched her every move. She could feel his gaze.

He slipped out the back door and she washed the dishes and set them aside to dry.

The sun was going down at the back of the house. It would be good to have Rosebud home, but she doubted James would want to give her up by now. Standing at the window, she remembered Jackson coming through the back trail, signaling her and how she had gone out and met him, his demeanor harsh, when now she knew him and why he had been unsettled and uncompromising.

His face appeared peaceful since the war ended. There were few slaves running for their freedom. The freshness of the loss of life and the state of war burned at the place where her heart sat. How could anything good come of all the death? She had no answers. She was overwhelmed with this new place in her own life. Mother and Jackson had saved her from the clutches of Mr. Rutledge. Had she been so foolish as to fall for his lies, she would not be here today, free, married to the man she was meant to be with. She shuddered.

Life had not passed her by. Mother was finally assuaged. Jackson was her husband, a man that would look after her. Father would love knowing that, too. And John. As a prayer of gratefulness passed her lips, she heard Jackson come in.

He washed his hands at the sink, took off his jacket and hung it on a hook. She watched as he looked at her from across the room and eyes locked on hers, walked slowly and stood in front of her. She thought she would die if he didn't take her in his arms.

She didn't have to wait long. Slowly his rough hands slipped around her waist and he pulled her close. When he kissed her, she felt like her legs would give out.

"Where?"

"Where what?" she was in a daze.

"Where shall we sleep?"

She thought for a minute.

"My bed is up in the loft. Mother's was in the small room downstairs. But Father and Mother's room is at the end of the hall at the back of the house."

"I never knew there was another room," he said.

"Mother shut it off after Father died and never went back in there again."

"Then that's where we will sleep," he announced. "Show me where this room is."

"But..."

"No buts," her husband said.

Karalee led him to the room, opened the door, and walked through. Jackson took her hand, shut the door and lifted her up in his arms.

Thirty-Four

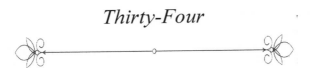

The next morning, still in a daze, Karalee opened her eyes slowly and stretched. She had been dreaming they were still on the train. She was alone. And yet for the first time in her life, she wasn't lonely.

She sensed Jackson wasn't in the house and lay back against the pillow, remembering. He had probably gone to Lily's to let her know he was back and to bring James here.

After a half hour lying about, she got up and dressed. Surely, they would be here soon. She whiled away the morning and made a bit of tea and eggs. There was little fresh food in the house.

What she wanted was a walk about the grounds, to see the land with Jackson at her side. It seemed surreal this house belonged to *her*. Father would be happy the house he built was not abandoned. Tears crept to her eyes. She may have the house but she didn't have Father or John.

Unsettled by the fact Jackson had not mentioned where he wanted to live, she prepared herself that he would want to keep his land, which meant she would live there. She walked the yard and checked out Rosebud's stable. It was clean, ready for her mount to return if, indeed, she ever would.

Everything she laid eyes on produced a memory: the gardens around the house, the verandah Father built the summer she was nine, John playing Hide-Go-Seek with the friends from next door who had long ago moved away. Wrapping her arms around her middle, Karalee walked all the way out back, remembering Jackson's visit the evening she saw his candle from her window, and then the dreadful winter night she went out and found him hurt. She had pressed her finger where the scar was. It would always be a sign of what could have happened. Karalee couldn't imagine losing him.

In time, she made her way back to the house. Another Michigan winter would soon be upon them.

She came in through the gardens, then the back door and heard knocking. Instantly her heart quickened and she ran to the front door wondering why he didn't just come in.

"Julianne." She opened the door wide.

"I heard you were back, Karalee." They embraced and Julianne stood back. "You look different."

Karalee felt her face warm. "Come, we'll have tea. I'll tell you all."

Julianne followed her to the kitchen, then to the parlor, Karalee carrying the tea tray. In a few minutes both sat in the matching chairs in front of the fire place, the room bright with mid-morning sun, tea cups warming their hands.

"Your mother stayed, didn't she?"

"Yes, she did. But Julianne, there was a terrible earthquake down there. That's why it took me so long to get home."

"I saw in the Cassopolis Vigilant something about it, but somehow I thought perhaps it was further away."

"It was devastating! The entire town is a mess, hardly a building left standing without damage." Karalee heard Julianne's gasp and went on. "Mother's house was shaken up but it survived better than most. I will never forget the floor feeling like water beneath my feet," she said and looked away.

"You've been through so much, Karalee. Yet you look happier than I've ever seen you."

Karalee lifted her left hand, revealing the wedding band she wore. Jackson had purchased it in Atlanta on his way down, knowing that if she was alive he was going to marry her.

"You're married?" she gasped and took her hand to see the ring. "A simple band. I love it. Jackson finally saw what he almost lost," she said smartly.

"You knew all along?"

"I could see it in his eyes every time he looked at you, and then how he walked away. You were the only one who didn't see it."

Karalee looked at her friend. "I guess I *didn't* see it. At least, not fully."

"Well, water under the bridge, so they say. Now, tell me how all this came about."

"There's so much to tell, Julianne."

161

Her friend pressed her lips together and waited.

"He never knew about his son, but...well, it's a long story, but he's with Jackson now."

"You're a mother," she whispered.

"Yes. I am."

"Oh my."

Karalee gazed at her friend and wondered for a moment if she, too, was not deceived. Julianne was a beautiful woman in her own right, yet she didn't seem to think so. Karalee expressed her thoughts aloud.

"I have had few chances and the one I had hoped for was not to be. It is my thought I'd best take whatever comes my way and be grateful for it. I fear above all things becoming an old maid and living alone. And since I have no brothers or sisters, I could not even be an Aunt. My life would be pointless."

Karalee saw her view. How could she make her friend understand her value...but then, again, she had not seen her own. She prayed a silent prayer for God to show Julianne how beautiful she was.

Julianne felt a jab of jealousy, seeing Karalee's contented face, newly married and a mother already, the very things she hoped for. She pressed two fingertips to her lips. "I have news as well."

"Yes?" Karalee's eyes widened. "Have you met someone?" she asked, leaning forward.

Julianne looked away for a moment. "Not someone new, Karalee."

Karalee tried to hide her disappointment. "Mr. Rutledge?"

"Yes, of course. Why ever not? I have had no other suitors and expect none."

"I'm happy for you, truly I am if that's what you want, Julianne. But I'm worried you will be a caretaker rather than a wife," she said softly

"I'm made for that. I am, at least, needed." Julianne looked down and sipped her tea. "It's a worthy vocation."

"You're right. You are needed. But does he need you for his *own* purposes or because he loves you?" Karalee could not keep quiet.

"I am not blind enough to not know he needs a wife to complete his favor to the public. He is running for a *very* important office.

162

Imagine me being a wife of the Governor of Michigan. Why shouldn't it be me?"

"You're right, of course," Karalee said. "It is not up to me. If you love him and are comfortable with that position, then God forbid I should hinder you. I'm sorry Julianne."

"Don't be. I've come to understand that life does not always offer love or turn out the way one planned. I am satisfied."

"How did he propose?" Karalee saw light come back into Julianne's eyes at the question.

"It was rather unconventional," she admitted. "As I was putting a letter on his desk that needed his signature, he turned and asked, *Would you me do the honor of becoming my wife, Julianne?* Since he is unable to stand I said I would think about it."

"Oh my!" Karalee's hands went to her mouth. "You gave him no answer? He is not the type of man to be slighted."

"I may look the fool, but I am certain I did the right thing by avoiding the answer right away. He is too used to that by his constituents."

"You were very wise."

They laughed together, drawn by the power of friendship.

"So may I ask, as your friend, will you accept?"

"I have decided, yes. You are the first to know, unofficially, of course."

"Then may I be the first to congratulate you." Karalee stood and held out her arms. Julianne stood to receive the blessing.
Jackson walked in the front door and smiled. "Julianne. How nice to see you. I take it you two have news by the looks on your faces?"

Karalee waited for Julianne to speak. "I have been formally asked for my hand in marriage."

"Who is the lucky fellow?"

"Mr. Rutledge."

Karalee saw Jackson's face. He tried, but failed to hide his feelings. "And you have answered him, I take it?"

"I plan to very soon. I'm going to make him wait a bit." She laughed nervously.

"As it should be," he said, went over, kissed his wife on the forehead, stood beside her and said, "I'm sure you have heard?"

"Yes, I have and may I congratulate you as well," Julianne said brightly.

Karalee wanted to burst with tears. She could see Julianne's face. Her friend was settling for something rather than waiting for the right one, but she must never let on.

"I must go and leave you two alone." Julianne pasted on her best smile. "But do not be strangers now that you are wed," she added for effect.

"Julianne, please let us know when you have more news." Karalee walked her to the door.

"I'm heading down to check out my place," he said and left the women to their talk.

Karalee let her friend out the door, turned her back and leaned against it. Her heart was sick. Sometime later she heard the wagon pull up at the front of the house.

"Jackson did you bring James?"

"Not yet. I haven't been out to Lily's yet. I wanted us to go together."

"Of course. I will gather my things."

Just in the door, Jackson pulled her back. "I know your mind is on Julianne. But she must make her own choices. Just as we must."

"I know. I just wish..." She stopped.

"That's why I love you." Jackson pressed her hands in his. "Because you love people the way you do."

She looked at him and couldn't help the tears that bubbled to the surface. "I want for her what we have Jackson," she leaned her head on his chest.

"As do I, but she must find out for herself. If she doesn't, she will lay the blame at our door."

"You're right. And it would ruin our friendship. I will pray that God shows her the truth."

"That's my girl. Let's go see Lily and pick up James."

Karalee needed to gather her own thoughts together. She would soon be a mother. All this emotion was wreaking havoc with her mind. A mother. Jackson's son. She could hardly believe it. And...she thought next, she hoped James liked her enough, to *be* a mother to him.

"Mind if we walk?" Jackson asked. "It's a nice day, leaves are starting to turn and we can talk about how to tell James. I can pick up my cart and horse to bring us back."

"Yes, please. I need some time to think about things. We have been rushing through these past few weeks. We've hardly had time to process all of it."

"That is true," he said and helped her with her shawl. "Don't forget your hat. The sun is bright today."

The wind blew softly and Jackson was in no hurry to move along, so they dawdled and discussed the matter ahead of them. Jackson would take Lily aside and tell her, and then together they would tell James they were married.

Karalee suggested he meet with James alone, in the event he was unhappy about it, but her husband refused. "This is how it is. James has had enough misunderstanding for one child. I want him to know he will always hear the truth from me, from us. The fact is, I let his mother down, created this situation. I should have been there. I won't make the same mistake."

Karalee nodded and admired her husband more, if that were possible. If parents would be honest even in hard times, and with their failures, children would be less inclined to think they weren't loved. She knew that from experience.

"You feel otherwise?" Jackson questioned.

"No, I think it right that truth between the two of you is imperative. I wonder if he will be disappointed that I have taken his Father away so soon, that he might resent me."

"You have a point."

"The thing is, dear wife, that you and I are the start of things. Like Julianne, we can't design our lives the way we think they should look, but deal with what is. We can never go back, but we can make something new."

Karalee considered that concept as she walked along. He was right.

She feared Julianne was attaining the goal of being married, but not achieving a happy relationship in the end.

"Jackson, he is your son, do as you think best. I have no experience in that regard," she said solemnly.

165

"And you think I do?" He laughed. "I am the boy's father and have no more an idea on to how to approach him than you. We are in this together. I'll speak, but I want you to back me up with your thoughts."

Karalee nodded. This was not going to be as simple as she'd thought earlier.

By the time they came to the conclusion they had *no* conclusion, they were standing in front of Lily's house.

"Well, we will work out our first dilemma together," Jackson said and knocked at Lily's door.

She came with a book in her hand.

"Jackson. Karalee. You're back. Come in," she said quietly. "I'm afraid James is still asleep this morning."

"And the book?" Jackson asked.

"Oh, I was reading through it myself to see if it were appropriate for his age."

"Thank you for taking care of him," Jackson said.

"We have had a grand time. Do you want tea, coffee?" she spoke quietly.

"Nothing. We want to talk to you first, anyway." Jackson headed for her small parlor.

Lily sat down, waited and knew the instant Karalee sat next to her brother, her hands twisted tightly in her lap. And...Lily noted a wedding band on her finger. She could hardly wait for them to say it and somehow managed to hold in her excitement.

"Did you have a nice trip back?"

"A very tiresome trip back. Things are much worse in Charleston than I ever imagined," Jackson told his sister.

"And your mother, Karalee?"

"She stayed behind. But she is well."

Lily nodded, wishing they'd get to the point.

"While I was on my way down, I...I feared that if Karalee was injured or worse, I realized I would be devastated," he started out with a glance at his wife. "And so when I saw she was well, I asked her to marry me. And she, well, we, did...get married."

Lily stood. "You married in Charleston? With all that was going on? I'm so very happy for you both, and I must say, it's about time."

Jackson looked surprised, Lily noted.

166

"I saw the way you looked at her, brother," she explained. "But I don't think Karalee saw it, at least not at first."

"I didn't," Karalee admitted. "I was too confused about Mr. Rutledge and my mother insisting I marry him. That, and the fact that I didn't think Jackson ever saw me as anything more than an annoying friend."

Lily laughed out loud. "Well, God worked it all out." She headed to the bedroom. "I'm going to wake James. He must know, too."

Before either could speak, Lily was gone to the other room.

Jackson stood and paced.

Finally, after some time, James, his hair still mussed from sleep, found a place on the settee, and waited.

Jackson sat down across from his son and asked how things went while he was gone, entering into the conversation slowly.

"I rode Rosebud every day," he said waking up a bit. "And we like each other."

"I'm glad you do." Karalee laughed lightly. "Thank you for taking care of her for me."

He nodded, scratched his head and waited, his brown eyes still showing signs of sleepiness.

"James, Karalee and I want to talk to you a bit about us.

"Are you married, Father?" he asked innocently.

"Well, yes we are. How did you know?"

"Well...my mom told me that people who are married have a ring on their finger. I saw her ring," he shrugged. "Then I saw you looking funny at each other."

"Funny?" Jackson asked.

"Yeah, you know, like you really like each other. Like that...like my mother and father..." whoops, I mean my other father."

"You can call both of us 'Father' if you want to," Jackson said quickly. "It's alright."

"You won't get mad?"

"Not at all. Are you mad because Karalee is going to be your new mother?"

Karalee noted his hesitation as James gave her a quick glance, then said. "No, I won't be mad."

"Then I'm not worried at all if you call Mr. Emory 'Dad' too," Jackson felt his voice give way.

167

James had to think about that for a minute. "So then you can be my mom while she's not here?" he said to Karalee.

"Exactly," Jackson said.

James got up, went over and hugged Karalee. "My mom said I was supposed to be kind to people and since you're going to be my mom..."

"Well, I think that's a very good reason." Karalee was overcome.

"Are you crying?" James asked, his face worried.

"Not because I'm sad, but because I'm happy. Now I have a boy of my own."

"Okay. I'm hungry, Aunt Lily." James stood.

"I'll get you breakfast." Lily went to the kitchen, calling out over her shoulder, "You two want to make it a family breakfast?"

Jackson looked to Karalee and at her nod, said, "Yep. Our first family breakfast."

Thirty-Five

After breakfast at Lily's that morning, James said he wanted to stay a few more days with his Aunt. He and Aunt Lily were taking a ride this very afternoon if he got his chores done. And he had chores for the rest of the week.

"Good idea, that one. Work first. Play later." Jackson ruffled his hair. "I'll be staying at Karalee's house and at my house during the day to work, if you need anything," he assured James and watched as he ran off to get dressed. "We have to muck out Rosebud's stall," he said as he flew by.

Karalee watched as he stopped mid-run and gave her a wave, then as Jackson and Lily talked quietly.

It seems James thought for sure Miss Karalee had given Rosebud to him forever. "We will settle that in a few days," Jackson said. "A boy can't think a gift is permanent unless there is an agreement: a gentleman's word, handshake, or signed paper.

To her mind, Karalee thought it a mere childhood misunderstanding, but her husband made it clear the boy had to know how to be a man.

As they rode the one-horse cart back to her house, she realized they'd had their first disagreement. She favored letting James keep the horse and Jackson favored returning the horse and perhaps earning it back through hard work.

"He's only eight," she'd said, to which he had replied firmly, "Eight is old enough."

She kept her peace. And then they'd turned to other topics.

"Since James is going to be at Lily's for a couple more days, why don't we go celebrate and eat at the hotel? I've got a few errands that need attention and we could use some things at the house."

So . . . Karalee thought, he intends to stay at her house for a few days from the sound of it. She knew he'd let her know they were moving to his place, if that was his decision.

"I do need a few things," she said quietly.

He had given her a look that she now recognized. Her heart beat a little faster as he hurried the horse on down the road.

* * *

Two days later, James came to stay with them at Karalee's house. Rosebud was back in her stall.

A pattern set in at *Mama's House*, as Karalee had come to think of their place, maybe because Father had built it for her. She watched fondly as James followed his father everywhere he went. He ate heartily and minded his manners at the table, and in fact reminded Jackson they should pray before they eat. "Mom said it's a good way to start dinner and to go to sleep at night." Jackson had looked to Karalee, who said a simple prayer every night.

More than once her heart had been touched when James brought her a fistful of wild flowers. And more than once, Jackson had done the same thing. She shuddered when she realized how close she had come to falling for Mama's desire that she marry well. Karalee *knew* she had married very well, and *that* only by the grace of God. She wanted James to have the same freedom and prayed she would be a good mother to him.

Lily came more often to eat with them and to see James. Karalee smiled when James wanted to go home with her for a night or two, saying Lily made the best cookies.

* * *

Three months passed before Karalee could wrap her mind around the fact that Christmas was one week away. Jackson had managed, with the help of the young couple staying at his place, to finish the harvest on time. Potatoes, carrots and onions had been packed in the cellar at his place and at *Mama's House* as well.

Soon the winter passed and spring was come again. Karalee wondered that she wasn't with child already, and then put the thought away. She had a son and James needed her. Jackson was busier than ever running from *Mama's House* to his place. But the good thing was the couple renting from him...were kind-hearted people who decided to stay on as long as Jackson wanted them. Karalee was glad it had all worked out.

Right after Christmas, Lily had met a gentleman at the church who rode into town looking for some men to help at his ranch. Peter Bond moved from Virginia in the middle of winter and everyone wondered why a man from Confederate territory was in Yankee country. No one trusted him, at least no one wanted to work for him, it seemed. The war was over but the hearts of men had yet to heal.

By the time spring had arrived, Lily had tired of the people at the church whispering behind their hands whenever he came through the door. He seemed to be a good enough man and even though he didn't attend regularly, Lily would see him at least once a month.

Finally, she walked up to him, when she saw that only the pastor took the time to say a few words to him.

"Mr. Bond, would you like to come to dinner next week? My brother has a house right here in town and if you'd like a good home-cooked meal, we'd like to have you."

He had looked at her for a long moment, she figured to see if she meant what she said.

"Ham, beefsteak and potatoes. Lemon cake for dessert."

She saw his mustache move; it couldn't hide his smile. "Well, when you put it that way..." He tipped his hat to her. "I'll be here next week, unless something comes up at the ranch."

Lily started to open her mouth to give him the directions to Jackson's house but he was already taking huge strides toward his horse. The man was tall; she could say that much about him. A moment later, Lily watched the dust rise up behind him as he trotted off. A man running a ranch had plenty to do, especially in the spring when the calves begin to arrive. She had heard folks talking that he had purchased a herd of cattle from a farmer in Van Buren County just north of Cassopolis. Word was that he had no family, at least none he had brought with him.

On the ride home, Lily announced she had asked him to dinner for the following week. Karalee spoke first. "We need someone to feed, with all that meat in the smokehouse. I'm glad you invited him."

171

"I've seen him down at the General Store," Jackson said. Karalee sensed he would say no more.

"I'll make up some of my special cornbread with honey on top," Karalee said as Jackson gave her a lazy smile.

Lily sat in the back of the wagon with James. Spring was budding out so quickly, Jackson said, "We'd better make the most of the time. We're planting more potatoes this year. Seems not too many folks around here grow 'em well and we've got good soil. Evan says we'll make more money and provide plenty of food for folks."

"I like the sounds of that," Karalee said. She loved the budding trees filling out the branches after a long winter, the smell of rain-washed earth, and the birds back from their winter homes.

James, like his father, was quiet. Karalee looked back as they rode along and saw Lily put her arm around his small shoulders. Neither spoke.

Life was good.

The next week was nothing but trouble, starting Monday morning. Jackson had come home saying Evan had broken his leg when he fell through the floor in Jackson's barn. He'd meant to fix that floor. But Evan would be no help until his leg healed. And Callie, his wife, was about due to have a baby. Karalee knew that meant Jackson would be doing the planting by himself. Also that perhaps the payments Evan was paying to stay at his place would not be forthcoming for some time.

"I should've repaired that floor," he mumbled when he came through the back door and told Karalee what had happened. "Doc fixed him up, but he won't be walking anytime soon."

Karalee watched as her husband run his fingers through his hair making it stand up around his head and as he reached for his favorite coffee cup and poured.

"It's time to plant. Maybe you'll be able to get some help." She offered.

"I'm looking into that this week."

It had passed so quickly, Karalee almost forgot tomorrow was Sunday.

"Company coming tomorrow if all goes well," she reminded him.

"Yeah. I forgot about that."

"Maybe Mr. Bond can help us and we can help him."

Jackson looked over at his wife, prettier than he'd ever seen her with her hair all whipped up on her head, and smiled.

Karalee's insides quivered at that look.

Thirty-Six

By the time Karalee had a moment to think, it was September again. Their first year anniversary. In the last few months, so much had changed. Peter Bond *did* come to dinner that Sunday and became a friend. When he learned that Jackson's main man had injured himself, Peter offered to barter one weekend at his place for one weekend at Jackson's place. "Two men working together get more done than one alone," he had said.

It didn't take long for Jackson to see part of the reason Peter hung around so much was because of Lily. A man may be busy, but he wasn't blind.

The dinner table at Mama's House was full every Sunday. Evan was walking around pretty well...still had to be careful Doc said, and Callie with baby Hannah, who was three months old, joined them.

The routine had become second nature to Karalee. Mama wrote only when she needed something, but said she was doing well and had met a very fine gentleman. Karalee's conscience bit at her, but her days were too busy to ponder the thought that Mother had moved on.

James was now the proud owner of Rosebud. He had cut and loaded wood for several months, and taken care of his horse, to earn the privilege of owning her.

Mr. Rutledge had not won the governorship in Michigan and vowed to try again next term. Last she heard he and Julianne had not wed. Karalee worried about her friend.

They had celebrated James' ninth birthday just last week. Ely Emory had come down to the celebration. He announced he was headed back to Ohio...his place here had sold. James was welcome to come and visit anytime.

The summer had passed so quickly, Karalee barely had a minute to keep up her journal. There was too much to write, but at certain times she forced herself to sit up in bed and pen several pages by candlelight, once Jackson had turned on his side and fallen asleep.

Karalee had not seen Julianne for weeks, with everything that was going on. She decided it was time for a visit and walked to town one Saturday afternoon and paid her a call.

As was her usual way, Karalee had sent a note to Julianne saying she would come around soon, to expect her mid-week.

It was a beautiful early fall day as Karalee started out walking the few blocks to town. Cocooned in a crocheted white lacy shawl around her shoulders against the slight chill in the air, she passed the General Store in favor of the visit first. It was near lunchtime and she hoped Julianne would have something prepared. She was famished and in her hurry had forgotten to eat. As she rounded the corner she noticed the Rutledge house seemed awfully quiet. The gardener was nowhere to be seen and the flower beds were untidy. Twice she pressed the huge lion head knocker into service with no response. Where were the servants? Maybe Mr. Rutledge had gone off for a vacation to retreat from the incessant work of running for office.

She walked around the back of the house. No one was working in the lush English gardens. Then just as she decided to try her chances at the back door, sure the kitchen staff would answer, she saw movement out of the corner of her eye, opened her mouth to speak and froze. She stared through an opening in the head-high bushes.

Mr. Rutledge was smoking a cigar. And he was standing, pacing in fact! Karalee barely breathed and blinked her eyes twice. Was she seeing right? Stock still, afraid to move lest he see her, she kept her eyes wide open. In a moment, he sat back down in his wheeled conveyance and entered through the specially made door from a slow rise ramp.

She let out a trapped breath, realizing she must have held it in fear. What should she do now? She pressed her fingers to her lips and made her way around to the front door again, and knocked louder this time.

Julianne came to the door.

"What are you doing here? It's so good to see you?" she greeted.

What was she doing here? Hadn't she received her notice? And where were the servants, Karalee wondered for the second time. One thing she knew about Mr. Rutledge was that he loved putting on airs and would never answer nor send Julianne to the door. It wasn't done in high-ranking houses. Perhaps he was downcast after losing the Governorship. She shook her head and wondered if she had actually witnessed him standing.

Karalee decided it best to play along. Something was afoot, but she didn't know what it was yet.

"I was in town and thought I might stop." Which was true.

"Come in. It's been an age."

"Yes, we have much to talk about." She felt her stomach rumble and pressed her hand to her middle.

"We were just about to sit down for a bite of lunch. Would you join us?" Julianne said rather formally.

"If you are sure you don't mind." Karalee wasn't sure who *us* was. There wasn't one person about except the two of them and Mr. Rutledge, because she had just seen him go in.

"I'll call Jasper," Julianne said and walked away.

Karalee took a seat in the front entryway, not wishing to overstep her boundaries and go walking about.

In a few minutes, they appeared: Julianne pushing his wheeled chair into the dining room where he greeted her with a fake invitation to join them for lunch. How in the world had she ever thought of marrying him? Karalee wondered.

"I'll get the soup," Julianne said quietly and walked toward the kitchen.

"Mrs. Woodridge," he said with a scowl, "I see that you have done quite well for yourself."

Karalee smiled and nodded slightly but said nothing. He knew she was married. He was up to his tricks again. This was going to be a terrible visit, likely not one she had hoped to have with Julianne.

"You look well," she said with a smile, ignoring his grumpy face.

"I am well. But then I'm sure you know I lost the bid for Governor."

"I had heard that, yes. Perhaps in a year or two you can try again."

Thankfully, Julianne came back with a tray, set up Mr. Rutledge's plate first, and then her guest's and finally her own. There wasn't a servant to be seen anywhere. The conversation was taxing at best, tiresome at worst. Finally when he feigned a headache was

176

coming on, he rolled himself into another room. Both heard the door slam rather hard on its hinges.

Karalee finished her soup and made light conversation until Julianne wanted to talk. The tension was palpable in the room when he was present.

"I am sorry for that." Julianne dabbed her mouth with a napkin and looked up.

"You have no need to be sorry. I came to see *you*," Karalee said quickly. "Shall we go to your parlor? I do love that room and have a bit of news."

"Oh, let's do." Julianne cleared the table and came back from the kitchen with a tea tray. Karalee followed her, chose her regular chair, and then watched as Julianne closed the double doors. She had never done that before.

"So tell me your news," Julianne said, eyes wide in expectation.

"I must first ask you to tell me what is going on in this house?"

When Julianne hesitated, Karalee asked, "Have your servants been dismissed?"

"Yes, every last one of them."

"What has happened? Could he be that destitute of funds?"

"No. He is angry because he did not win the election and everyone is paying. He released half the staff for good, and the other half is off for a fortnight."

"Ah, so you will have at best a skeleton crew for the household for some time then?"

"As it seems. He is moody, as you know, and blames everyone for any folly that occurs. Two of the young girls dropped dishes while guests were here, they were so nervous. He sent them packing with no notice."

"My friend, do you think you should leave? Do you feel threatened in any way?"

"Not like that." Julianne said quickly. "I have my work here, taking care of him. And he pays me well."

Karalee almost blurted out what she'd seen in the back gardens, but forced herself not to speak of it.

"He will no doubt call them back, apologize, and things will be like they were," Julianne said softly.

As Karalee reached for another cookie, her third, she tried to decide whether or not to share her news. It seemed rather unkind to speak of joy with someone who was dealing with such hardship.

"You have made me wait long enough. Tell me all." Julianne leaned forward in her seat.

It seemed proper to take her friend's mind off her troubles and speak of good things.

"Well, as it is I'm going to be a mother, again."

"Karalee that is wonderful! When shall we expect this new family member?"

"March will be the date as far as I can figure. That's what Doc said, too."

"I'm so happy for you! What does Jackson think? Or does he say much?"

"He smiles."

"He smiles?"

"Yes, I see in his eyes he is pleased. He is a man of few words, you know."

"That I do. I remember...oh, speaking of Jackson's family, I'm so happy for Lily, too. Do you expect Mr. Bond and Lily will form an alliance?"

"An alliance?" Karalee said lightly.

Julianne nodded, unaware of how businesslike that sounded.

"Time will tell," she answered her question with a slight smile.

For the next hour, Karalee and Julianne shared memories, walked back in time from the difficult days now behind them and all they had learned.

The conversation slowed and Karalee announced she should be going. There was much to do at home.

"Julianne, has Mr. Rutledge spoken of marriage recently?" She decided to bring up what she most dreaded: Julianne's connection with this man.

"He has not," Julianne said truthfully.

Karalee could see the hurt in her eyes.

"Perhaps you should prepare yourself. He is not marriage material. I am so sorry to say it to you," she said, and saw Julianne stiffen. "That is not to say at some time in the future he may be, but as you can see, when he does not get his way he can be very difficult."

178

"I have seen it," Julianne admitted.

"Then you are aware. I will say no more."

Karalee knew what a good marriage looked like now. Her parents had one, as long as Father did what Mother wanted.

Then she mentally scolded herself. Jackson had shown her his commitment, his dedication and most importantly to her, his defense—both of her person and her emotions. She had loved her husband most when she'd sounded, even to herself, like Mother and he had not punished her, but shown her love instead.

Suddenly it occurred to her that Julianne likely knew little of this. Her father had first gone off to war and she, an only child, was left to care for her sick mother. She had been everyone's caretaker. And so she easily adopted the role with Mr. Rutledge. Karalee felt her ire raise and stood. She had to leave before she told her friend Mr. Rutledge was a deceiver of the worst possible kind!

"I must be on my way, but I promise you, I will come again and we will chat. Sooner this time," she said with a sad smile.

"Do come again. It does get lonely here and without servants around..."

At Julieanne's shrug, she said softly, "Don't worry. I'll be back in a few days." She hugged her friend and walked out the door.

On the way home, she collected her thoughts and knew she had to talk to Jackson. Tell him what was going on and ask him what she should do. She was not afraid of Mr. Rutledge, except in one way; he could so easily deceive. She needed her husband's advice on the matter and went straight home, bypassing the General Store.

179

Thirty-Seven

Within minutes, Karalee was in the house and searching for Jackson or James. Both were gone, then she saw the note, written in James' fine hand; that they were down at the farm shucking corn.

Karalee knew shucking would be an all day job, so made her way to the kitchen, buttered a slice of bread, added a spoonful of strawberry jam and wandered through the house, eating. She stopped at the library. Father's books had been brought in from the stables and placed back on the shelves. James was already reading from them. She found, to her everlasting delight, that James loved to learn. And that he favored history and architecture. Karalee ran her hands over the spines as she walked along, glad that Father had instilled in her the love of reading. Perhaps it would pass the time until she could speak to Jackson.

She had long ago started a novel called, The English Queen, found the small piece of paper she had used as a bookmark and began to read. That lasted about an hour and she found herself struggling to stay awake. The sun burned through the window, warming her face. She closed her eyes, rested her head against the wing of the stuffed chair and promptly fell asleep.

The next thing Karalee remembered was a door shutting. She jerked awake and grabbed at the book that nearly slipped off her lap. Jackson was home. She sat still for a few moments and listened to him as he moved through the house—the sound of his boots dropping to the floor, and as he washed his hands then scrubbed his face with the cotton towel nearby. He would come looking for her. He stopped in the kitchen and drank, parched from the dust and the fields. And then, she knew, he brushed his suntanned hands through his hair and smoothed it. He had been taught to come inside clean. She loved that about him, how she could predict his every step.

She sat quietly. First because she wanted to let him find her, and secondly she was so tired, it seemed as though her arms had no muscles...she just couldn't move.

A soft smile came to her face when she heard him come nearer, and then as he spoke her name.

"I am here."

He came to the door, leaned against the doorway and gazed at her for a long moment, walked a few steps and pressed a kiss on top of her head.

"I have done nothing worthwhile today," she admitted. "I'm sure you are hungry. Where is James?"

After a pause, he said, "I am hungry. And James is staying with Lily tonight." He winked.

Karalee smiled and offered her hand. Her husband drew her up into his strong arms.

"Then we shall make the most of it," she said, slowly pulled from his embrace and went to the kitchen. A hungry man was a nuisance. It gave her a reason to get up and get going. She was tired so often these days.

Much later that evening, Jackson sat with her on the sofa. "You have something on your mind."

"How did you know?" She looked into his eyes.

"I know you. Something's bothering you. What is it?

Karalee scooted closer and he put his arm over her shoulders. Then she told him the whole story about what she'd seen. She knew he would think before he answered a weighty topic, so she waited.

"You know, for I have told you enough, Rutledge is a deceiver. Julianne is unwise to be under the same roof with him without servants. He does not care to protect her reputation, as you see."

Karalee hadn't thought of that.

"If you want her to come here and stay, there is plenty of room."

"Jackson, she wouldn't leave him. She's not like that."

"She must have a backbone, else she will find herself in worse trouble than she is in now," he said firmly.

"I agree. But she does not know he walks. I saw for myself...not as a cripple, but like anyone...he paced, Jackson."

"Tell her."

"I know I must, but I'm afraid of what she will do. She might defend him and then what? We will have pushed her closer to him, rather than away."

"Tell her before she is married to the man! Do you want me to tell her?"

"No. She would rather hear it from me."

"Then do your duty, Karalee." Her husband got up and walked down the hall to bed.

At first thought, she was offended. You ask a man a question and he gives you an answer. He doesn't consider the ramifications. Especially when it comes to women's sensitivities.

Then she gave it a second thought and realized what he said was true. If she loved Julianne she would do her duty, even if it caused her to be angry. Their friendship would survive it.

That decided, she retrieved a bowl of butter from the cold storage, put it out to soften, and went to bed.

Tomorrow she would go and tell her friend the truth. But for tonight, as she pulled her nightgown over her head, she prayed God would give her the words and climbed into bed.

Jackson pulled her into his arms without a word.

* * *

Karalee had barely slept. She ran ideas through her head as to how she should present the information to Julianne: for sure, not in Mr. Rutledge's house. She had formed a plan. Up before sunrise, she made pancakes, slathered them with the softened butter and poured maple syrup from the Wiggins' farm in Vandalia onto her husband's plate. He was surprised to find her up and awake at dawn, when he normally rose.

"You've had a bath." He snuggled her from behind and untied her apron as a tease. Her husband loved morning, she normally did not.

"I couldn't sleep so I took a long bath." She smiled when he nuzzled her neck. "It was time…dust was smothering me after a rainless week and my hair was so dry." He grabbed her waist and pulled her toward him, then retied her apron.

"Are you complaining woman?"

She couldn't help but laugh. "Eat your pancakes before they get cold. You will need your strength."

"And so you must have been awake all night forming your plan. Going to share it?" He stopped and gave her a look as he poured his coffee.

"Do you want to hear it? More eggs?"

"Yes and yes."

Karalee told him the idea and he approved.

"I prefer you do not go into the man's house."

"Indeed, I do not like being there," Karalee assured him, "especially knowing there are no servants about. I can only imagine how Julianne feels."

"Get her out of there. If she doesn't want to come or Rutledge makes a fuss, send a note by courier. I'll come at once."

She smiled at her husband and had no intention of calling him in, unless absolutely necessary. Jackson came close to despising the man. She didn't blame him, but no need to start another fracas. War had taught her that some disagreements were not worth dying for.

It was settled. Jackson made her promise she would not enter his house. She made the promise, and saw her husband off. He had kissed her silly until she wanted him to stay. Fanning herself with her hand, she shut the door behind him and put on her best shawl. It was time to visit the General Store. She wrote her list, said a prayer for God to give her strength and to please stop her if she was not to go through with it.

After all her items were bought, she paid a bit extra for the courier to carry a missive to Julianne immediately inviting her for lunch. Then he was to drop off her purchases at her house this afternoon. He was a new boy who seemed quite pleased to do her bidding.

She had already sent a note with Jackson for Lily that morning. Hoping all would fall into place she walked home. Famished, she sat down to eat a chunk of ham with a biscuit, even after that pancake breakfast she'd eaten earlier…reminding herself she ate at the crack of dawn and it was eleven o'clock, after all.

All she could do was done. Now she would wait. Karalee picked up her knitting and tried to keep her mind busy. The baby would need a hat and sweater since he or she would be born in a March snowstorm, no doubt.

Karalee laid her hand over her belly, waiting for the day when she felt movement. "Like a butterfly flutter," one of the ladies had whispered to her. "That's how mine felt the first time."

James would learn of her condition later. She and Jackson wanted him to have as much time with James as possible. Julianne was the only other to know, plus Laura's mother whom Karalee had confided in when she thought she might be expecting.

Her heart was full, except for the fact she had to tell Julianne the truth about Mr. Rutledge today.

She shooed that thought away, knowing it was sinful to worry. The warm sun fell across her face again. She laid her head back against the soft chair and promptly fell asleep.

A good stiff knocking at the door woke her. She stood too quickly and had to stand for a moment until her head quit spinning. It was the new boy, whom she learned was Walter Case. His father was a new doctor in town. This was Walter's first position. Karalee gave him a generous coin and sent him on his way. He ran back explaining that her goods would be delivered later.

Nervously she opened the note. Julianne was coming. She had agreed to the tete-a-tete. Even now Karalee's lemon cake lay cooling from the early morning bake.

Lily, Julianne and Karalee were going to drive over to Vandalia to get early apples. The afternoon would be spent peeling and making applesauce at Lily's. She had all the equipment. The new Mason Jars with wax sealers were just the thing.

Since Lily knew nothing about the situation, Karalee thought it wise that she and Julianne could discuss the problem on the way home. That way they would have spent some time together and enjoyed each other's company for an afternoon.

Karalee put away her knitting, stepped down the hall to their bedroom and changed into an old work dress, dark navy with gray trim. It would due for picking apples and canning all day.

The plan worked perfectly, and by the time the applesauce, still warm, was packed up in wooden crates, Julianne was her old self again. Lily had been excited to have company about her place; the day had flown by. Thus far things were working out.

184

Once they were down the road a ways, Karalee asked Julieanne about the sewing store she dreamed of opening one day.

"I had nearly forgotten about that," Julianne admitted.

Karalee heard the wistfulness in her voice. "You know *Parm's Place* closed since old Parm moved away. I think Jackson would help you turn it into a nice little place. I'm sure the family could use the rent money now that Parm left, what with their sick daughter."

"Do you think so?" Julianne turned her head.

"The building is for sale. Jackson said something about buying it. It's right on the corner."

"I barely noticed it."

"Why don't we drive by? It wouldn't hurt."

Karalee turned the horses around, pulled on the reins as the cart came to a halt in front of the empty building. "Shall we look in the windows?"

The two of them shaded their eyes and peeked in the dirty windows. "Looks like the perfect size," Karalee said.

"It does have a large glass case there."

"How would you set it up?" she asked Julieanne.

At her shrug, Karalee thought she'd best get to the point. They were already in town and she had planned to speak while they drove back.

"I have a position," Julianne said as they climbed up. "I should get home. Dinner will need to be done, but I do thank you for the afternoon and the applesauce."

Karalee turned the cart and headed down a nice leafy lane. "Julianne, let's go to the field and pick some wildflowers. I need something pretty in my house and so do you."

"What do you mean?"

"There's something I need to tell you. You're my friend and I can no longer keep this to myself. I must ask you to listen and consider what I'm saying. Agreed?'

At Julianne's nod, she continued. "I sent a note last week telling you I was coming to visit, but you were surprised, which means Mr. Rutledge did not give you the note. Further, no one answered the door, so I went in the back to use the kitchen entrance only to find him out in the gardens. He was standing on his own two feet,

Julianne...in fact, pacing. He sat back down in the wheeled chair and came in as though a cripple. He is *not* a cripple!"

Her friend turned with accusing eyes. "Of course he is. I help him every day."

"He has been deceptive all his life. If you knew all the details, you'd pack your bag and come stay with me and Jackson, this instant."

"I will not leave a man who needs care," she said. "Turn around, I think I've heard enough."

"I must mention one more thing. Julianne, do you see he is ruining your reputation? There are no servants in the house. It looks very much like you are his kept woman."

"I thought you were my friend."

Karalee pushed down the desire to blurt out more information and realized her friend needed to process what she'd already spoken, so turned around. "I do not expect you to understand immediately. I would be shocked, too, to learn all of this if I were you. I was almost taken in by him, as you well remember."

The quietness surrounded them, interrupted only by the waving of leaves in the trees over their heads, the idea of wildflowers forgotten.

When they pulled up in front of the grand house, Karalee couldn't help but remember the night she had almost been fooled into a marriage that would have ruined her life. She had to say one more thing.

"Don't get down, you're expecting. I'll carry the box in," Julianne said firmly without looking at her.

"Why don't you ask Mr. Rutledge if he will come out and get it?" Karalee knew the words were wrong as soon as they left her mouth.

"I will do no such thing."

"I'm sorry, Julianne. That was unkind. I'm just so angry he has deceived you."

"I will survive. I always do."

Karalee hated the sadness in Julianne's voice. "Please remember what I told you?"

"How can I forget?" Julianne said as she walked away.

Thirty-Eight

Karalee turned the wagon around, feeling a tightness in her stomach and accusations in her mind kept creeping up. What right did she have to tell Julianne what she should or should not do? She always hated when Mother did that to her and immediately began to doubt her motives. Maybe she had overstepped her boundaries.

She parked the cart in the front yard and asked Laura's brother to unhitch the horse, feed and water him. Jackson had forbid her to do anything that might injure her or the child.

The afternoon was spent in sheer misery. She had failed. Failed to get her point across in kindness, failed to stop her tongue from accusing Mr. Rutledge. Talking to herself, she said, "What? Should I have just let it go? Said nothing, watch her fall and then look in her eyes and wish I had spoken?" She answered her question with a firm, "No!" and worked out her frustration pulling weeds in the flowerbed.

Jackson found her thus. Dirty dress, dirty face and soil under her fingernails. "I have gloves on the bench out back," he mentioned.

She shrugged.

"So I take it things did not go well with Julianne today?"

When she didn't answer and kept digging, Jackson went through the back door, finished cleaning up and looked in the ice box. He ate cold biscuits and ham, opened one of the new jars of applesauce, which he knew he'd hear about later, then went back and took a bath. She needed to be alone.

Some time later, he heard the front door close. He was in the office now, finishing paperwork.

Later, he heard her soft knock and almost laughed out loud when he saw her eating the last biscuit in one hand with a hunk of ham in the other. He guessed she wasn't in the mood to cook either.

"I made a big mess of everything." Karalee sighed and sat down.

Jackson turned his chair around and waited, knowing you can't rush a woman.

In time she confessed all and sat dejected.

"You can't fix the world. As long as you told her the truth, that's all you are responsible for. She will make up her own mind."

She didn't say anything.

"Why don't you take a bath? You'll feel better. You didn't overwork yourself did you?"

"No, not like that." She stood slowly.

"I'll be about a half hour here. Meet you in the parlor about eight?" He saw her glance at the clock as she walked out.

Jackson couldn't help but smile. She wanted to help people but took it personally when people were being hurt and she couldn't do anything about it. He loved that about her.

Later she came, tied up in her nightclothes and wrapper. The fire burned low. It had been warm for the last day of September.

His wife would worry until there was news, so he tried to make conversation but she seemed content to knit. After a time, she opened up.

"Jackson, we stopped and looked at *Parm's Place*. I mentioned that you were looking to buy it. Do you think if Julianne does come away, she may be free to use the space as a sewing and tailor store?"

"Was that her idea or yours?" he asked quietly.

"Mine, pretty much."

"We could talk about that," he agreed with her. "Best to wait and see what she's going to do."

"You're right."

She went back to her knitting.

Jackson changed the topic. "James is ready to start school. He's a bit late. But now that harvest is almost done, he can attend."

"I'm glad. He loves to read and I think he will do very well in math. He likes to draw, too."

"I've noticed. When I ask him to work alongside me, he seems to have a good sense of what is coming next. I'm real proud of him."

Karalee smiled, her knitting resting in her lap. "Thank you for hearing me out, Jackson. I know things will be all right...at least, I hope they will be.

"They will be," he said and got up, kissed her on the forehead and voice low said, "Come to bed. You're tired."

"Soon, dear." She set aside her knitting and yawning, rose to her feet, made preparations for tomorrow's breakfast, and then followed him to bed. She was asleep before she could think another thought.

Jackson didn't move when she came in and smiled in the dark when her soft snore reached his ears.

* * *

Four days later Jackson came through the door. "Karalee."

"I'm in the office," she said distractedly.

"What are you doing up on that ladder?" he grumped.

And before she knew what was happening, he had grabbed her waist and set her on the floor. "I was putting books away."

"James will do that task. You should not be taking chances. What if you fell and I was not here?"

She actually hadn't thought of that.

"I have news." That always got a woman's attention.

"News?"

"There's someone outside who wants to talk to you." He nodded toward the door.

"Who?"

"Go see for yourself," he said.

"Julianne! What are you...you have your bags..."

"Karalee, I confronted him. He raged and I felt like he was going to strike me. He got up from his chair and stood!" She burst into tears.

"I'm so sorry," Karalee said and drew her friend inside. "You will stay here."

"I feel so foolish. I'm still shaking from the quarrel."

"It just happened?"

"Yes, just now. If it wasn't for Jackson going inside to calm him down, I doubt I would have come out of the house in one piece."

"Jackson was there?" She glanced at her husband who stood in the doorway.

189

"Yes. Walter, the courier boy, had come to the door in the middle of the mayhem and heard the shouting, ran back to the General Store and then Jackson came."

"How glad I am that he did. Come sit down. I'll get you tea."

The dining chairs were pulled out and a cup of warm tea was between Julianne's two hands – hands that were still trembling.

"He didn't even knock. He must have heard Mr. Rutledge raging at me. He was saying horrible things. Horrible things..."

"It's all right. You're here and you're safe."

"He was so crazy that he rushed toward Jackson and would have hit him, had Jackson not held both his fists. But your husband did not hit him, even though he had the right to. He just pushed him to the floor, told him what he thought of him, and told me to pack my bags. And to take my time."

Karalee smiled at that and Julianne took a deep breath and heard her husband's booted feet on the wood floor as he walked away.

"We will work this out. Now go on up to your old room. I'll make dinner and you can unpack."

"I just threw everything in," she admitted and stood. "I need to be busy," Julianne said and paced.

Karalee called for Jackson to carry up the bags and when he came down, pulled him into her arms. "I'm so proud of you."

She heard him chuckle deep in his chest, her ear resting on his strong shoulders.

"A man has to do what a man has to do." He held her tight against him.

"Yes, but you do it so well." She ran her fingers through his hair.

He stepped away. "I'm hungry, woman." He growled next to her ear, as he rained kisses down her neck.

Karalee wasn't sure what kind of hungry he was. She pulled away, gave him a look, and tied on her apron. "We have a guest. I'll get dinner." She heard a low chuckle as the back door shut.

Thirty-Nine

March 1868

Karalee heard the front door open. Finally.

"Jackson, hurry, please hurry. This baby is not going to wait. Go get Doc."

Jackson heard the desperation in her voice.

"You going to be okay?" He asked from the doorway.

"Yes, but you must go. Now!"

Jackson heard a low groan from the bedroom as he hurried down the hall and out the front door.

He and Doc were back in an hour, but by that time, the baby had come. A lusty cry came from the house and Jackson felt fear grab his insides. Doc pushed past him and there on the bed lay a baby, red, and squalling.

Doc slammed the door in his face and said to wait outside. Jackson heard crying for a few minutes and then nothing. Just low talking. What in the world was taking so long and had the baby..." he tried not to think about that.

Instead, he did a quick replay in his head. Julianne was down at the store and Laura had gone off to school, so there was no help to be had. That, and the fact he had to saddle his horse and the March winds were dead set on holding them back...Jackson was angry. They had taken too long.

He paced, got a drink of water, his ear hoping to hear some squawking. When the door opened he was standing next to it.

"Jackson, come in and see your son."

"Son?"

Doc looked at him. "Well, it was either that or a girl."

Karalee was so happy, she could have died right then. All was well, Doc said, and she had delivered a son. Doc waved and said he'd be back tomorrow.

She looked at her husband and thought perhaps he was going to fall to the floor. His face was as white as Mother's French lace tablecloth.

She patted the side of their bed. "Sit down." Karalee pulled back the blanket and showed him. "This is your daddy." She felt tears pop up out of nowhere. "You'll make him proud won't you?" she said to her son.

Jackson stared at the baby and then caught her eyes. "Was it bad?"

"For a little bit, but I had been having pains all day, I just thought it would take longer. Doc said the first ones usually do. I guess he was just ready," She shrugged.

"So, you're okay and he's okay?"

"Yes, we're okay. Why don't you go get James?"

Jackson stood, glad to be busy. I'll be right back." His horse was still reined near the door. He pulled his hat down lower over his face, knowing he'd be riding against the wind, went down to Lily's and hauled James home on the back of his mount. "You have a brother," he said. Lily said she'd come another day, she was not feeling well.

"A brother? Yankee Doodle Dandy!" James exclaimed and whooped to the wind.

Had anyone told him two years ago he would be here at this place, with a wife, a son, and now another son, Jackson would have called them a liar straight to their face. Life had a way of changing a man's plans. And he didn't mind one bit.

* * *

"We'll call him John Henry Woodridge," Jackson declared after a few days went by.

Karalee looked up from bed while feeding her son. "You'd like to name him after my father and brother?"

"Would you like that?"

"Of course, I would. "I wasn't sure if you wanted him named after you or..." she stopped.

"I would never name my son after my father," Jackson stated firmly.

192

"I love you Jackson Clay Woodridge," Karalee said. "Every time I call John Henry I will think of them both." Tears ran down her face in buckets, just like they had for the last four days. Everything seemed to make her cry.

"Well, it's settled then. James and John."

"And Jackson." She smiled.

"You'd better get used to us." Jackson kissed his wife and went out to cut more wood. "Winds are whirling around like a hurricane out there."

Karalee could only rest. Their household was about to change. James was in and out of her room between chores. Jackson had taught his son the value of work and taking care of people, animals and possessions. She, on the other hand, had insisted James go to school as much as possible.

Pleased and satisfied in her role, she looked down at John and kissed the top of his soft, dark head. Just like his father's and brother's.

"Aunt Lily will be here soon so she can hold you. I must get up and move around," Karalee whispered.

It was late afternoon, but the dark clouds and heavy snow made it feel like bedtime. Julianne came in, stomped her boots and declared the entire county was at a standstill. She had not had one customer all day.

* * *

Jackson, Evan, Walter's father Dr. Case, and the preacher from the church had come to help finish up *Parm's Place* for Julianne's new shop. Jackson had bought it outright and turned the back into a storage space, while renting the front out to Julianne. She had done quite well when some of her former customers had returned. It would take time to get ahead, but she was free from the clutches of Rutledge's evil hold.

Jasper Rutledge had been forced to return to work. He assumed he would be Michigan's next Governor and had resigned his position at the bank. He now worked as a teller rather than a manager. And word around town was he was in danger of losing his grand house and had already lost his license to practice law.

Karalee was not happy about that. But he had brought it on himself. She shivered at the thought she had almost been caught in his web of deceit, which reminded her to be thankful for her husband.

A letter arrived from Mother congratulating her on the birth of her grandson and inquired instantly, hoping Doc had *not* delivered her of the child.

There was no need to explain. Karalee set the letter aside and only then realized the return on the envelope stated she was now Mrs. Major Charles Montgomery.

Julianne came in and took the baby while Karalee managed to bathe and dress herself, after nearly a week of lying about. It was good to be on her feet again.

Once the beef roast was put in the oven, carrots and potatoes peeled and added, she quickly washed out the dirty nappies and hung them to dry on a chair near the oven. And then she heard John Henry crying.

She went to feed him while Julianne changed her bedding and they chatted.

"He's just the perfect little bundle," Julianne gushed. "I'm already in love with him."

Karalee was so happy; she wanted Julianne happy, too. "Think you might want to have children someday?"

"Oh, probably not. Time is running out and I'm so busy at the store. I used to dream of it, but now I have other dreams."

Karalee nodded and decided to step lightly and bring up another subject.

"Have you seen much of Dr. Case? I hear he's quite a good doctor and handsome, too."

"He's been very nice. He does good work, too. My glass display case is beautiful. When you can, you must come to see it," Julianne said.

"I can't wait. I hear he loves doing carpentry work when he can manage to find free time. He has been here almost four months now. And attends church."

"Yes, he does." Julianne kept working.

"Do you...do you...?"

"Now don't you go meddling, Karalee," Julianne said sharply. "I have work to do and no time to go out and about with a gentleman if that's what you are thinking."

"I don't think it's just me thinking...." She left that hanging.

Julianne stopped smoothing the sheets over the bed and gave her friend a stern look.

"He has shown no interest, and if I have learned anything, it's that the man must do the asking." Julianne thought that should settle the matter.

"Then you must be blind."

"Like you were with Jackson?"

Karalee smiled, "Yes. Like that."

"Don't go stirring up things. You've got enough to do without managing me....although I will admit that if you hadn't stepped up and told me the truth about Mr. Rutledge, I would not be as happy as I am today."

"Well, at least I am good for something."

Julianne shook her head.

"I hear Dr. Case is looking for an assistant."

Karalee knew that would get her attention.

"Oh?"

"I talked to Walter the other day and he is not interested in following in his father's footsteps. Blood makes him sick to his stomach and he's useless anytime someone is hurt, which are *his* own words by the way."

"I have my life and I'm staying right where I am."

"Okay..." Karalee knew when to stop.

* * *

In July there were two functions the first Sunday of the month at the church: John Henry's dedication that morning, followed by a wedding. Miss Julianne Johnson and Mr. Daniel Case found they had more in common than originally thought. They were married in a simple ceremony and a potluck was had by all. Just as the folks had finished eating, the most of them anyway, a sudden gully washer from the sky sent them all home, none expecting it.

Forty

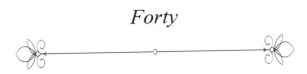

James Clay Emory became James Clay Emory Woodridge by law that same month. He rode in the wagon, holding his little brother, and announced he was going out to clear some space near the woods out back, if no one minded. He had an idea to build a miniature farmhouse for his brother when he was old enough to play in it.

Jackson encouraged James to build whatever he saw fit and the two of them worked on it whenever there was a spare moment.

"He's got the gift of working with his hands and visualizing a project. Good with math, can run up a list of numbers in his head in no time at all," Jackson told Karalee one evening at dinner after the boys were in bed.

"I love the way you teach him…and John Henry someday," she whispered, overcome with joy.

* * *

One year later, Doc delivered Julianne of a son. Three weeks later, Karalee was delivered of a daughter.

Jackson asked Doc to stay for dinner. He accepted. "That little gal gave your wife a hard time. Her fists were stuck under her chin. Mom will need a few more days to heal this time," he said swallowing hot coffee and eating as quickly as he could."

"She sure did. Karalee was worn out. But she's a pretty little thing."

"Prettiest baby I've seen in a long time," Doc winked and stood to his feet. "But don't repeat that." He warned. "Might get back to the other mothers."

"What's the hurry Doc?" Jackson asked.

"Got word about an hour ago Mrs. Smithers is going to be needing me. But it's her first and unless she's like your wife with John Henry, it'll take her a little time."

Jackson didn't envy Doc's job and said so.

"Well, it's about time for me to retire. Dr. Case is a good doctor, a lot younger than me, too. I'm hoping we're going to change places, me taking the slow road for a change."

"You've got it coming to you," Jackson agreed. "I'll pack some bread and cheese and get a couple apples out of the cellar to send along.

"Thanks. That'll help. If she slows down and I'm stuck there, it'll be good to have something to hold me over." He laughed and was out the door ten minutes later.

Jackson went back and peeked in the door, after leaving Karalee and little Emily Kathryn Woodridge to themselves for a little while. They were both sleeping.

Karalee gave her daughter Mother's first name as a middle name. Even though Mother would probably never appreciate the gift, she knew her daughter would one day come to know she was named after her grandmother.

Later in the evening, Doc came by to check up on Karalee and brought word from Julianne. "Dr. Case returned from Kalamazoo just in time to learn he had a son." He smoothed his mustache and shook his head.

"Was he upset?"

"Yes. He would have liked to deliver his wife, but alas, babies come when they're ready. Walter is fifteen now and this will likely be the doctor's last child."

"I know Dr. Case is a few years older than Julianne but he has been a wonderful husband. She has loved running his office."

"Yep. She sure seems happy. I was glad she chose to close out her sewing business so Dr. Case could open his office there."

"It's been a good thing. Folks can come to him now whenever possible. It saves him a lot of time," Karalee said.

"You're telling me. My back is worn out from riding all over the county," Doc admitted. "Times change and I'm retiring."

"When?"

197

"Promised myself when you, Julianne, and Mrs. Smithers delivered, I was done."

"Really? You waited for us?"

"Yep. It's official. Dr. Case is top man now. I'm going home and whittle little birds from wood branches."

Karalee wanted to hug him and tear drops fell. Partly from relief because Emily's birth had been more difficult than John's and she was tired, but most of all for Doc.

"Doc Case will be right down the street from you. It'll be all right." He patted Karalee on the shoulder, took a peek at the baby and walked out the door with his black bag. Somehow it broke Karalee's heart. She wept all afternoon and could not explain to her husband why she couldn't stop.

* * *

What seemed like days passed in years. On Emily Kathryn's second birthday a letter arrived in the post. Emily walked early with a little help from her brother John Henry who was already three. She wanted to follow him around and found she could do it better if she walked. She had barely crawled before she was up walking. Karalee had her hands full chasing the both of them.

The household had grown, and now that Julianne was nearby, Karalee stopped by to visit her and William Lincoln Case, *Will* for short. Big brother Walter ran errands for his father and took care of the office whenever Julianne had to feed Will.

The visits with Julianne became more work than pleasure. Emily and Will got into everything. What one didn't think of, the other did. Karalee had to keep the visits short.

She never tired at the joy of seeing Julianne's face as she held her son and cared for Walter as her own. The fulfillment Julianne had always wanted was now hers. It was downright inspiring. Both of them had come too close to making the wrong choices in their younger years.

And both were equally determined their children would not be forced into situations they did not want. Only time would tell if it could be managed, because as they soon learned, children had minds of their own.

198

Karalee said her goodbyes and stopped at the post. Emily needed a nap and Jackson would need a break. He had taken three-year-old John Henry with him for the day.

Once inside the house and both of the youngest children asleep, Karalee sat down and went through the small stack of mail. Bills to pay, orders for potatoes, and then the last, a letter from Mother, only it wasn't in her handwriting.

She set the mail aside for Jackson, opened the missive and found only one page. She quickly turned it over and saw another signature, flipped it back and started to read.

Your mother is ill. She has been abandoned by her husband and is now here ...in Paris. Please make arrangements. Send funds. I will see she gets passage home.

What? Karalee couldn't wrap her mind around the words. Was this real? Quickly while the children slept she asked Laura's youngest brother, Lawrence, to ride down to Jackson's place and hand him the letter. "I wish to know how I should respond. I'll send a wire today, if he thinks it appropriate." She shooed him off.

It took overlong, or perhaps she just thought it did. John was awake playing in the parlor and Emily still asleep when she heard Jackson ride up. That means he thought it necessary to come...which made her more frightened.

"What do you make of it?" she asked instantly.

"Did you know she was in Paris?"

"No."

"And I see the letter is not in her hand. *Her husband abandoned her,*" he read.

"There is a name on the notice. A man's name. Why didn't she write? She must be ill, Jackson. Shall we write or wire? He said Mother is ill. I cannot go to her," Karalee said firmly.

"No you will not. If anyone goes, I will go."

"But what about..."

"We'll worry about things as needed. Right now, send a wire, asking more details and we will respond."

"All right." Karalee checked her husband's eyes. He wasn't as distraught as she was. That calmed her. She could see a fierceness in him if he thought something was wrong, so nodded and sent him back to work.

Emily woke, so she fed her and set her atop a pallet on the floor nearby and wrote the letter. It was ready. There was nothing more she could do.

* * *

It took almost two months to get word back and that with Dr. Case's help; he had studied for two years in Paris, so he knew the right people to address. He took the time to transcribe Karalee's letters into French so there would be no misunderstanding.

Karalee learned that, indeed, the man Mother had married was not the man he said he was…he used her money to take himself to Paris and abandoned her there. Some kind soul who knew the man's reputation for deceit took her in.

By the time Mother arrived, she was thin and bedraggled. The trip across the ocean had nearly done her in, she admitted. Her beautiful dark hair, now more gray than black, was unkempt and her clothes were secondhand. Karalee cried when she saw her. The light in Mother's eyes had gone out and so had the determination. Her limp was disturbingly worse…she walked with a cane.

Karalee settled her into the small room off the dining room where she had stayed before, the one James had been staying in. She moved him up her brother's room in the loft..

At first, too ill for the children to visit, Mother had kept the door shut to her room. Dr. Case had come by and said sadly there wasn't much to be done. He gave her powders to help with pain and left.

Overwhelmed, Karalee managed to care for the children during the day while her mother slept. Jackson and Dr. Case sent correspondence abroad, trying to find the man who was her husband. Finally, word had come back. The handsome, debonair man was being brought back to America, charged with marrying multiple unsuspecting wealthy women, relieving them of their fortunes and moving on. Jasper Rutledge all over again.

It would take months to investigate and likely none of Mother's money would be recovered. The house in Charleston was returned to the bank, having received no payments for more than a year.

Mother's beloved family home was gone. Karalee was glad she was not well enough to know all of that. Everything she had lived for blew away like ashes in the wind. Life had a way of slapping one in the face. Her thoughts were on the edge of bitterness when it occurred to her...life was never fair but the choices one made determined more than one realized. Her own choices, for instance: working with Jackson to free the slaves, even though Mother didn't approve, choosing Jackson over Jasper Rutledge, and more.

Indeed, there were hard times, but there were also good times. Karalee knew she had to find a way to reach her mother.

"Mama, are you awake?" she asked the moment she had a chance to sit down with her. "I've brought tea. Your favorite, Earl Grey. Would you like to sit up and have a sip?"

When her mother moaned and tried to sit up, Karalee realized how little time they had. "I'll help you."

Karalee settled the pillows and without much help from her weak, frail body, was able to get her mother into a sitting position. "Shall I open the drapes just a bit and let the sun in?"

Mother nodded.

"Two cubes and a spot of cream." Karalee stirred and handed her just the cup, knowing she couldn't manage the saucer, then took up her tea, clinked it against her mother's cup and said, "To us."

Mother had actually smiled a little. Her blue eyes were cloudy grey now. She had been asleep so often Karalee had hardly seen them. It made her want to weep, but she knew she must not show her emotions or Mother would know.

Forty-One

The next morning, Mother looked better, so Karalee asked if she might bring in Emily Kathryn.

At her nod and after a bath, she brought a sweet smelling, wiggly little girl and put her next to her grandmother. Mother, who was sitting up, had a half smile.

"She's named after you, Mother. Emily Kathryn."

Tears fell slowly, first from Mama and then from Karalee.

Thin, bony, trembling hands caressed Emily's cheek and then her mop of dark curly hair.

"Snuffle," Mama whispered.

Karalee smiled and cried at the same time. "She doesn't like dresses, Mother. Especially blue ones," she added.

Suddenly, Mother looked tired.

"Here, I'll take her. Tomorrow we'll visit with John Henry."

"John Henry?" Mother asked, voice hoarse.

"Yes, you remember. We named our son, John Henry."

"You did?"

"Yes." Karalee felt sad she didn't remember. Perhaps it was too much. "Mother, you rest. I'll bring you something to eat in a little while." She settled her in bed and shut the door.

Jackson came and the crew found their seats at the dining table, Karalee telling them Granmama was sick and to be very quiet.

James and John Henry were quiet, Emily Kathryn had found her voice and loved using it. No amount of shushing her seemed to work. James finished his food and took her outdoors for a walk in a miniature wagon Jackson had made. Thankfully, Karalee could finish her meal and took a small plate into Mother, but she was asleep.

Dr. Case came by the next morning and said not to worry if she didn't eat. Folks in bed and ill didn't require as much food to keep them going.

Later in the afternoon, Lily had come down to take the children to her house so Karalee could catch up on work, and have a visit with her Mother without interruption. As soon as the wagon was out of sight, Karalee whipped up Mother's favorite dessert—apple pie—and baked two of them. While they were cooling, Karalee sat down to a quick breakfast of tea, toast and cheese. Mother was especially attentive this morning and looked as though she might rally.

"Is your tea hot enough?"

She nodded.

"Mother, do you care to talk about what happened?"

At first Karalee thought she hadn't heard.

Mother started talking and didn't finish until she had told the whole story. The man had come dancing into her life and swept her off her feet. He was handsome, debonair, well-dressed and could dance like a dream. "He did not smoke cigars," she added. Soon enough he had proposed, Mother accepted, and they were married in St. Michael's church. He had then moved in and promised a trip to Paris.

"I was never more in love," she whispered.

The words stung Karalee.

"But he was another Jasper Rutledge," she said bitterly.

What could she say? It was true. Karalee nodded for her to continue.

"I was sick and he knew it. Instead of helping me, he sent me alone to his brother's house when I arrived in Paris, saying he would follow. He had taken my money and left."

"I'm so sorry, Mother."

"I deserved it."

"No, you didn't." Karalee disagreed. "No one deserves to be treated that way.

"I was never happy," she spat the words. "I was always taught that we were better than everybody else. That changes people, Karalee. It gives them feelings they are more worthy than others, that the world should give them adulation. I have found out myself, it is not true."

"You are right, Mother."

"For the first time in my life, perhaps," she said with a little laugh. "But as you see, here I am."

203

"Yes, here you are. More tea?"

"I believe I will."

Things were smoothing out.

"Is that little Emily Kathryn around?"

"No. She's down at Lily's with the boys. She quite loud and boisterous."

"Let her be," Mother said firmly. "I blocked you in when you were a child, tried to prepare you for the life I wanted for you. It was wrong. And don't say it wasn't," she put up her hand.

"You and Jackson know how to raise children. Don't think I haven't noticed. I was too busy trying to find my own happiness and now it has eluded me."

"You still have time," Karalee suggested.

"You and I both know I don't. That is why I'm sitting here with you now while I feel good. I want you to know I wish I would have been a better mother and wife. Father and John would still be here, if I had."

Karalee remembered their conversation before.

"For all the times I was wrong, I am sorry. But in spite of me, you made it. For that, you should be grateful. I was never an easy woman to please."

All of it was true, but there was no need to repeat what Mother had said, so Karalee listened.

"Further, you must make sure you lay me next to Father. He may not forgive me for that, but then he won't know, will he?"

"No, he won't."

"Now, no tears. I'm tired from all this talk. I'm sure I need to have a talk with God, so I will shoo you out. Don't go rounding up the children, either. Go to your room and take a nap."

"Yes, Mother."

Karalee stood, straightened her Mother's pillows, set a glass of water on the side table and said, "Rest now, Mama."

"I will Lee-Lee." She heard as she shut the door, went straight back to her room, pulled the coverlet over her head and wept.

Jackson came in later and found his wife asleep on their bed and Mother asleep in hers. He could smell those pies, though. Quickly, before the children came back he set a pot of beans boiling, cut a large hunk of ham off the shank and added it to the pot. By the time everyone was back together, Karalee could make a batch of cornbread and they could eat those pies.

Back outside Jackson cut wood. The trees were starting to turn again.

Forty-Two

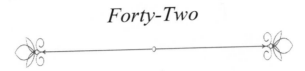

Three days later Karalee knew it was Mother's time. She told Jackson as they sat at the dining table before the kids were up.

"I'll take the kids down to Lily's," he said.

"No, I want them here in the house. I want Mother to hear them, not to feel alone," she whispered. "I can't have her feeling alone."

Jackson nodded. "I'm headed out, rest while you can."

He came back with his coat on and took her in his arms, "I know another baby is on the way."

"How did you know?" She sought his eyes, the eyes she loved so much.

He just smiled as he held her close.

Karalee never felt more loved than at that moment. He kissed the top of her head and she heard the back door shut quietly.

She and Mother had had their talk. Made their peace. There was nothing to be done now. Dr. Case said she would rally near the end, and she had. Time had formed a fragile bond, but death held the key that would end it.

Karalee had sat with Mother and talked to her, told her not to worry. She would be fine. Sometime later the clock struck ten in the foyer and she could not leave Mother even though she was gone. In a daze, for death never seemed permanent until it actually finished its work, Karalee stood and shut the door. Tears would not come. They didn't need to. All was said that needed to be said.

James came by while she was in the kitchen, washing dishes. "She's gone, isn't she?"

Karalee nodded and twelve-year-old James threw his arms around her middle. She embraced him and smoothed his hair, his face hidden in her shoulder.

"You're thinking of your mother, aren't you James?" she asked softly.

"Yeah, I guess I am. Now you've lost yours."

"Yes, and you know just how it feels, don't you?"

"Yes." He slowly disengaged himself and said, "But we won't forget them."

"No, we won't James. God won't let us," she said through tears.

"I'll go get Father."

"No, let him come at lunch. He'll find out then."

"Okay," James said and went out back to find comfort with Rosebud.

Karalee opened the door one more time and went in. Mother lay in soft repose, her hands at her side. She had never wanted them crossed over her midsection, she said half a dozen times in the days before.

A smile rested on Karalee's face. "Mama, we didn't always see eye to eye, but I know you tried your best. This will always be *Mama's House*. I'll do *my* best to keep it in the family. I'll see you on the other side."

Epilogue

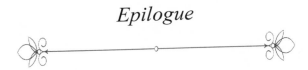

Mama was buried next to Father and John in the Prairie Grove Cemetery on Penn Road in Vandalia.

Early the next year, Matilda Mae Woodridge was added to the family. She came just like John had, quietly slipping into the world when Jackson was working the fields. She was their docile, quiet child. The entire household loved Mattie. Everyone said she had Karalee's dark eyes.

James left home too early to Karalee's liking. He was studying architecture and had traveled to Paris last summer, the first to leave. John Henry was his father's son; he loved farming and inherited Jackson's family homestead. Three generations of Woodridges were raised there.

Emily Kathryn, strong-willed like her namesake, bought Mama's House and kept it in the family for two generations. Matilda Mae married a Boston attorney and moved away. Her great granddaughter, Geneva Jane, attained *Mama's House*, the last family member to live there.

If you push back the brush from the headstones at the tiny cemetery near a Dogwood tree, you can still see Jackson and Karalee's stones sitting side by side.

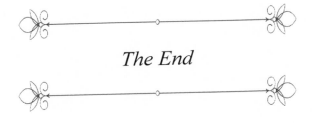

The End

Books by Patricia Strefling

Edwina
Cecelia

Beyond Forgiveness

Ireland Rose
Rose's Legacy

Cadence

Wedgewick Woman

Stowaway Heart

Lacy's Lane
Lacy's Life
Lacy's Legacy

Robbi
Robbi's Redemption

Hush Mama
Mama's House

Coming Soon...
Make me Forget

Contact Info

Dear Readers . . . I always love to hear from you!

You give me great insight as to what touched your heart. I enjoy hearing stories about your life. Please feel free to share your heart. You may want to leave a comment or just have a chat. God bless you!

Connect with Me Online:

https://www.facebook.com/patricia.strefling.author

http://www.patriciastrefling.com